D1521361

ORIGAMI
STRIPTEASE

PEGGY MUNSON

suspect thoughts press
www.suspectthoughtspress.com

Copyright © 2006 by Peggy Munson

Cover design by Shane Luitjens/Torquere Creative
Book design by Greg Wharton/Suspect Thoughts Press

First Edition: October 2006
10 9 8 7 6 5 4 3 2 1

Library of Congress Cataloging-in-Publication Data

Munson, Peggy, 1968-
 Origami striptease / by Peggy Munson.
    p. cm.
  ISBN-13: 978-0-9763411-9-2 (pbk.)
  ISBN-10: 0-9763411-9-0 (pbk.)
  I. Title.

PS3613.U6934O75 2006
813'.6--dc22

                                              2006002529

Suspect Thoughts Press
2215-R Market Street, #544, San Francisco, CA 94114-1612
www.suspectthoughtspress.com

Suspect Thoughts Press is a terrible infant hell-bent to burn the envelope by publishing dangerous books by contemporary authors and poets exploring provocative social, political, queer, spiritual, and sexual themes.

I want to graciously acknowledge the following people, without whose practical, spiritual, and emotional support this book would not have reached print: my amazing family (who hopefully won't be embarrassed), the queer folks who formed my personal village people (starting with Matt K., my first gay friend), and my friends with MCS and CFIDS who inspired me with their courage and art. To Mayra Dole, Nicole Reinert, Katherine Devoir, Michael Druzinsky, Billie Rain, Erin McElroy, and Sharon Wachsler, who all offered particular insights (or dirty words) reflected in this text. Special thanks to Noelle Kocot for helping carry so many wooden cows, and to Emily Dings and Johnny Carrerra for packing the U-Haul (and more). To Ian Philips and Greg Wharton, who help origami yearlings become proud gay mooses, and the other editors who have supported my work, with special thanks to Tristan Taormino and Susie Bright. Thanks to the MacDowell Colony, Ragdale Foundation, and Cottages at Hedgebrook for their faith in me, and to Alicia Goranson for organizing readings. Thanks to my early writing teacher Diane Vreuls—who showed me how to locate my own weird voice. Thanks to every cowboy-gendered soul I have befriended or loved, and those who petitioned to be Jack. Here's to a wider world of gender, best stated by my cowboy friend Tuck who really does answer the question "Are you a boy or a girl?" with the answer, "Nope, I'm a cowboy." And to a non-ableist society of wheelchair accessible, sign-interpreted, fragrance-free spaces: let's dismantle the barriers already!

An excerpt from *Origami Striptease* originally appeared in *Outsider Ink* (www.outsiderink.com), Spring 2005, Sean Meriwether, ed.

Origami Striptease is a
Project: QueerLit
contest–winning novel.
(www.projectqueerlit.com)

This book is dedicated to Rachel Samet and Abe Doherty
—the sunniest sunflowers I know.

CONTENTS

Part I:
The Ice Hotels

1.

One day, Jack quit moving his cock, and the world just stopped.

That motion, deep in the boiler rooms of desire, had moved the hands of Greenwich Mean Time. It moved all hands. It moved hands passing money, and it moved whores trading hands. Jack's cock was the sole reason my poppy opened. Jack's cock was the morning headline every morning, for months of screaming paperboys, and then it halted. The presses screeched. Grinding cogs and sooty smells of newsprint fled their tired rooms. My body lost its conch shell sound of oceans. My body was The Hole: a place where prisoners are thrown into solitary confinement.

"Stop right there. Stop right there and genuflect," I said to another boy dying to be my jailbird.

I couldn't remember where he came from or why I agreed to make him happy for a night, but I was lonely. In my head I wrote a hundred letters to Jack. In my head I begged like a bullied child. I wanted to roll over and lick Jack's boots, but I grabbed the boy's collar and choked him as I pulled his head down. I made sure he smelled the hours of wait and need trapped in my pussy. I liked to hear a boy barely able to breathe between my legs. Sort of like a death rattle, his desire.

Part of any person is camouflage. The key is to know which part. With Jack, the parts were card tricks with a million variations. He was a con artist in leathers. He'd make me drive the car and sit shotgun acting totally uninterested, yet think about the way I stroked the wheel and quivered like a go-go girl behind glass. He made me beg for a sip of his soda and then he gave it just to watch the way I sucked. He liked to see me work a straw. My lips were just a crystal structure forming around Jack. I'd lie in bed with one cock bobbing in my mouth from gravity and one stuck in my pussy, and I'd think about him until I gagged. Each cock was a prosthetic when it wasn't his. Each cock was just a ruse.

"Stop there until I come," I said. The boy obliged me with his tongue.

For months after he left, it was a pall of quiet. The night tried to clear away onerous lies to make way for flapping clotheslines. Street-sweeping trucks made their hovercraft noise, filtering into the still drapes of my sleeping neighbors like elephant infrasound. A month went by, then years. People said their serenity prayers. And then Jack's letter came.

"I'll be there in twelve days," it read. "To figure out the koan: does love come free? Does Freelove know? I want to see you; meet me. —Jack."

I sat there like a paperweight upon my bed and held my yearning down. Of course, I'd heard that he was dating someone else (the grapevine isn't all that long—I knew she was a painter, and I hated her for being so enticing). I guessed he would be buffered by a gorgeous girl. Alone, he'd be afraid that I would call him on his fears or open up my awful wells of batting eyes. "Why, Jack?" I'd ask. "Why did you run?" Jack's too afraid that every girl's a sinkhole if he gets too close.

He'd stand there like a block of ice, crate-trained and docile, his words enclosed in a cryonics facility somewhere. His clammy hand would grip the new girl, a girl perfect and artistic, with Jackson Pollock shoes of manic paint splashes. She would hold onto Jack like a lost dog she'd just found in a parking lot, with flawless timing and a taut leash. Jack would look at me like I could never understand the way that scissors-legged women draw him in. Those tiny cuts the women make in folded paper to reveal two melded hands. I'd never get it, how he needs to be so pruned.

It's my own damn fault that Jack has never known

the way I feel for him. Writers can't speak fast enough; that's why we write. No utterance has the exactness of the printed word. "You're so restrained," some people say, until I write them poems. I tell them to admire a comic book if they want "Wham!" and "Blamo!" Scissors are the kind of muse a guy like Jack believes he needs — the kind he thinks will make exquisite corpses out of words and not write ransom notes. He doesn't know how much I'd pay for him, and do, and will. I would pay any ransom to release him.

But who am I to judge his Stockholm Syndrome anyway? It's not like I have never been a willing captive. It's not like I have never yearned to be so worthy of a thief. To be so wanted, and so chosen. It's not like I have never loved a person who possessed me. I sometimes need a con to trick me into feeling. I need a con to see the gambler's tell in how I clench my kings or twist my ring. To overturn my nervousness and sneak me into backdoor clubs of intrigue and of catastrophic loss. What do we know about ourselves until we're duped into believing we have lost control?

And maybe it was Jack who tricked me. "Close your eyes," he said. "Just trust me. Here." His hands had taunted everything, like keys on kite strings. "Here." His hands had made me feel like I was just a little virgin, dumb and inexperienced. But I was glad to close my eyes, so glad. If I looked straight at Jack, we would have played an archetypal game, a game of cowboys and of maidens left behind. Of horses and abandonment. Of weathered quilts and galloping suspenders and suspense and creak and freedom. I could never last another round of that.

"Come on, Jack," I said. "Stop the games. I know you love me so make love to me."

I hated how squeaky I sounded, like a burnt projector ruining the whole illusion. There was no place for a woman like me in those old movies Jack liked. I was too direct to be demure. In chiaroscuro, everything about me was eclipsed by women who had learned the rites of cigarette holders. Those women knew to drawl a moment out. They knew the game and reveled in it. They sat there passively and never felt like mice. Those women made a guy feel ten feet tall. Those women lived their lives within director's cuts and never felt directed. They were doing all the growing and the cutting.

Those women didn't notice Jack's parameters, how he had been idealized by my pen. Jack said, "I can't make love to you. I can't. I can't do that."

"Why not?"

"I can't," said Jack.

Jack made me beg. We dated six long weeks (it seemed like months) and still, my boy would not capitulate. We watched the hazy burnished sun. The skinny moon. The days collapsing all around us.

Clouds appeared like telegrams. It felt like everyone was dead. We welcomed an Apocalypse each time we kissed. We weren't afraid. We kissed there on a grassy knoll and heard the swells of locusts in the humid hour of freeway cars. The world around us was a series of assembly lines. I was intoxicated. Jack was rolling me around; his cock was pressing up against my leg. His cock was speaking its own language, one of stratospheric need. His cock was trying to find a way to tunnel out, and in. His cock was taking me into its prison, pulling me, his conjugal, with vicious dogs that yapped away at freedom barking dark staccato at the moon.

"I need it," I told Jack. "Please let me. Please."

The stripped pincushion of the sky played voodoo with my heart. And Jack was growing rough with me; his hands had turned to thrash and grunt. His hands were children raised by wolves. His hands were gently violent. But they were disassembling, not just ripping. His hands were noble savages, stumbling into church to seek redemption. My body, stiff as pews, was broken down by stained glass that had dappled me in colorful celestial lasers. I was being crushed into terrazzo walkways. The word, the body, blood—they crushed me into color. They crushed me into Jack's religion. Before I knew it, there I was, just kneeling, begging for his cock.

I had to have Jack's cock.

I had to have the body, and I had to give it blood. I had to have the bloodless symbol, bloodless body, there. I had to pull the blood from each Siberia into that point, the laser point, to rip and cauterize and rip. And that's when need had turned to hunger. There I lay, my body pressed against the grass, and I was drunk on chlorophyll, and I was Jack's to sacrifice. But he just poised himself there, stunned it seemed, his eyes becoming rotaries of gambler's silver balls and anniversary dates. His eyes imagining a world of rational addictions. His balk was all it took for me to pull him down on me. I pulled, and Jack remembered where he had to be. But then he seemed confused. "Come on, Jack, please." I said. "I need you, baby. Please."

The liquid motion stopped. It was like I had suddenly become the girl inside that interactive pen, the girl you can undress by tipping it one way, then dress by tipping back. But I was simply naked, naked in a pen.

"Not now," said Jack. "Not now."

The real pen sat upon my desk. The pen was filled with fluid. Jack had given it to me. On nights when I had writer's block, I'd sit there tipping back the pen. I'd watch the girl undress, and dress again. I'd think about the whorish stories I would like to write with it. Some days the pen, engorged with fluid, was the fistula inside my gut that yearned to drown me from the inside out— because when I did not, and could not, write about him, I just swirled into the hollow drain of self that called me into loneliness.

PEGGY MUNSON

The naked pen had cost him next to nothing. I dangled it in front of him one day. "I want you to adopt a starving child," I said to him. "Sign here." I showed my belly for his signature. He wouldn't sign his name on anything. I took his cock out of his pants and sucked until I felt the acid in me rising up. I didn't care how many holes were rammed or carved or burned. My need for sustenance was so particular that I could rarely get it filled. His hips, his hips, his hips, moved like those cranks and rods on wheels of locomotives fueled by steam. We churned there, both of us, into the greatest robbery there ever was. And no one witnessed anything. Jack always got away without a witness.

"Not now," said Jack. "But later. Later when it's fully dark."

One time the Perseids had rained around us. Wishes, falling stars, a plethora of wishes. "Now," said Jack, his cock against my leg. The meteors, Jack's kisses from my shoulder blades to hipbones, gluttony of wishes. His cock, toy engine fueled by geysers, there, my conjugal, so perfect sliding in.

I put his letter down. I lay there tipping back the pen, then stripping off my clothes, then playing with myself between the covers:

> Me, the girl undressing in a tube, the girl behind the plastic of a naked implement, trying to fuck myself the way that Jack fucked me. Me ripping off my clothes. Me tearing at my underwear. Me talking dirty to myself. "You little whore, you little bitch." Me piling pillows on my bed so I could hump them. Me having rodeos with cotton batting. Me trying to find a dick that's big enough, or hard enough, like Jack. Me riding dicks on top of mounded covers. Me trying to

stop myself from coming. Me trying to slow the climax. Me trying to keep illusions going. Yes, the light is perfect. Yes, the trail of silk goes on and on where I have walked. And yes, the man beneath me is a woman, tinted noir.

I came so hard, Jack, harder than the steel-tipped ink that filled the pages you once left. But god, where were you? God. Twelve days.

2.

I pulled the mailbox door and saw Jack's letter crammed against a Chinese menu with a typo, "stying blam" for string bean. The words themselves were staring at me through a sty, weird eyes from everywhere when all I wanted was to hide. It had been two weeks since I left the hospital. I smelled like rotting daisies from the cold white rooms that had soaked readily into my flesh. I huffed on oxygen so that I wouldn't smell my sickly skin. The world became a yellowed photograph awash in turpentine. My former partner had moved out with all of the belongings but a cast-iron pan left mockingly upon the table, and my clothes and bed. Looking at the pan, I thought of people waiting for an execution, their hands around signs that said "fry, fry, fry." I wasn't sure if I should put the pan away or leave it out. Jack's letter jarred me. It reminded me of how my life had been before, back when I entertained a constant stream of tricks.

I had been semifamous once. Yes, during days of decadence and simple pens, I ushered boys into my home. I mixed them drinks with made-up literary names, then let them fuck me. I wrote the scintillating details in a wire-bound book I called The Cherry Vault. I sold the writing to slick magazines like *Bully* and *(Ero)genous* and *Spanky Smacky Spam*. I didn't know of Jack, had not been tempted by his transcendental lust, and I was happy with my life of cheap confessionals. "You want a Naughty Peregrine?" I asked the one with slick pomaded hair. Some liked to seem like roughnecks and drink white trash booze. Some liked to sip a good martini from a glass that looked exactly like an upturned skirt. They rolled off of my tongue as easy as clichés, these boys.

"You got any Colt 45?" West asked, his fingers tap-

ORIGAMI STRIPTEASE

ping out a bass line on my old Formica countertop. These boys — they wanted to pass, but not too much. Each date took on the aura of a 1950s reenactment, with a drape of costume and the posture of taboo: We chose our fucking palette from a misspelled menu, making intimate nonsense that took on meaning of its own. The boys had mediocre goals but I still oohed and aahed for them. "I'm saving up to buy a pair of thousand-dollar cowboy boots that tell the story of the Alamo," West bragged. He wore a rockabilly shirt and jeans that were as stiff as two Marines on Flag Day. He took a comb out and swirled his hair into high surf while I bent over in my dress to check the crisper drawers for booze. I knew this boy would fuck me like a country song, with lots of bottle slide and teardrops in his throat. He pulled me up against his polyester cowboy shirt and ran his burlap hands across my back. I kissed him desperately and sucked his lower lip. "I need it little cowboy, now," I begged. West had the kind of lips that always tasted like an old tin cup. The kind of lips that turn your petty change to scrap. "You like to rip the bandages off bandits, lady?" He held my tit within his hand as if perplexed that it was not a lid to something else.

"Sure do. I always have." They never said it outright, that it hurt to be a boy. They never let me know the metaphysics of their aching balls, although I felt a migratory ache that traveled through my hideout caves like outlaw wanderlust. I knew it came from them. I had it too: the need to fuck. I was a mindless cow pushed by a metal prod. I loved the way a simple shape could do me in, the puerile fuck geometry. West started showing me his treasure map of scars and then he hitched his crotch and squeezed his balls and told me there was "gold in them thar hills." I reached out so that I could touch his pack and then he said, in country twang, "Uh-uh, don't tell me that you're just another buzzard circling dry gulch looking for a home."

"A buzzard doing what?" I wanted it so bad, that simple shape.

He rolled his eyes and threw the cowboy accent off. "Just suck my dick, and never, ever touch me without asking first."

They liked my drinks, but lipstick was their drug. They always bet on red and ended up in black. They gave me what they had—their cocks—but we both knew I fed them pomegranate red. A short skirt and the oldest pinup poses made them hard. "Hey! Duck. Duck. Goose!" I said, and flashed my cotton-covered ass at Sam. Down at the trailer park named Whimsy Hollow, Sam poked his pink flamingos into rubber cones and made a slalom course out of his street. "We're in the pink again," he said, and grinned at me. His drunken buddies used the cones to test if they were too drunk to drive home. They weren't mean drunks, but good boys who liked tipping back a few on weekends once they'd cleaned the grease off of their hands. This was a transitory place, but when I watched them weave, it had that solid sense of home you only find in places where you know the residents will never get away. I loved those thin walls of the trailer and the way the kitchen angled to a bow so that the house felt like the inside of an ark. I had a sense of how economy had trapped us all. I had a sense of the endemic leash and its ironic freedoms. There, we turned to animals, two animals on zoobreak wandering outside our bounds.

Sam's hands knew everything about an engine, and it showed. He pried up into me with concentration and endurance, then he wiped his hands off on a rag beside the bed. He even used mechanic lines like "Give me time, I'll have you humming." There were multicolored whirlygigs above his bed that spun while he was nailing me. The whole room was infused with tacky beauty, beauty that reminds you how to be a hopeful child. He had a lamp made from a bowling pin, and Betty Page pajamas. When Sam talked, he quoted Shakespeare or Jim Morrison, and the complexity began to make me like him way too much. He didn't trifle with sophisticated gear around the bedroom. There were holes behind the bed that he had knocked into the paneling with other girls and those I used as handles when he slid his fist inside of me. He tamped each piece of body memory to fossil fuel and that was why, revved up and fucked so well, his girlfriends always turned into the seamstresses of highway lines. He waved his melancholy wave beneath the carport strung with tiki lights, a Coors Light in his hand. Sam was the best fuck in the world, but he would likely spend a lonely life beneath a Mustang hood. "Why can't it work for us?" he asked, a plaintive sigh, but he knew why. My hands began to fit too well inside his wall, and I was scared I would become imprisoned there, within that hopeful tacky beauty.

"I'm sorry, baby, but at least you've got your flock," I said, and kissed him by the pink flamingo course. Like everyone, I had to mosey on. No sooner did I wave goodbye than I was writing sordid stories in The Cherry Vault.

We're all familiar with the shape of hours, and that's why cramming feels so great. I loved the urgent stuffing of one thing into another thing. I liked boys who were young but acted like they only had a month to live. I liked to feel them punch my clock, the way they rose up to the tyranny of walls. Mitch had an egg timer inside his fertile mind. "Let's just get down to business," he said, setting down his Perished Letter Office (made with a twist of lime and mint), and grappling for my top. He muttered foggy words and pinned me to a wall so I could feel the pressure in his jeans. They all had fools' gold in their pants, but somehow it was better than a million-dollar brick. These boys, in general, were not long on words. I didn't care if their suave posturing broke down to lisps between my legs. I liked to see composure turn to sweat that dripped onto my naked hips. They had to understand that they were there to tweak my clitoris and not to talk about the Bible, Sartre, or a family recipe. They had to understand that they could not assume a thing with me, and I would not assume their gender ID or their kinks. Mitch made me spread my pussy with a shoe horn and he licked me like I was a sugar maple tree. Some people have a way of turning moments into nectared distillations. Mitch was a chef who could spend hours on one cream sauce, who turned the simple elements of roux into culinary ecstasy. "I like to stir," he always said, and shrugged when asked about his work. That's what it felt like when he slid his tongue between my legs, like he was stirring the foundation for the richest French cuisine. Some boys had chivalry of big arms that would never let a tumbling woman fall. Mitch, on the other hand, would never let a soufflé fall, and he would never let a woman starve. Curled up with him, after the act, he kissed like he was leading sow to trough again. "Dessert?" he asked, and pulled me onto him.

My hunger was the worst. I'd felt it since the day I noticed there were no boys in my town, and then I wandered to the outskirts and the borderlands, until my clothes were ripped from journeying and throat was parched—and then I saw the bounty that was there. I thought they were mirages, shimmering and stoic boys who packed their pants with incandescent heat. Just as the particles from the sun are twisted on magnetic lines into the northern lights, but only in the margins of the world, the sky lit up with stage lights where these boys appeared. Outside the edges of the careful grid, I could be fed. I hadn't known the borderlands existed. As far as I could tell, the world was flat and dropped off in a cliff dive at the edge of town. But when I walked that night, until I reached the outskirts of the city and the bars, I saw them: boys. Drag kings and trannies, daddies, gender-freaks and butches, all decked out in suits and jeans and hanky codes. They waited there so nonchalantly, knowing I would come.

"I'll be your past-due lullaby," Deke said, gulping his Unspoken Vowel (with vodka—naturally—and coconut creamed in a juicer), and I sucked the cum right out of his imagination down my throat. They knew I was a literary tattletale and some of them crammed all my words so far back in my throat they knew I'd never excavate. The first time I met Deke, he didn't wait for courteous hellos. He dragged me to the bathroom, sat me on the toilet seat, and shoved his cock into my mouth, like he'd been driving with an urgent telegram between his legs. "Go on and suck it, pig," he said, and grabbed me by the neck. He told me that he took me there because he planned to fuck my mouth so hard that I would puke, and he did not like cleaning up disgusting vomit from a pig. "Glory, hole-ih-lu-ya," he sang, sliding it between my lips. They had one thing in common, all these boys. They loved it that I never could be filled. They loved it that I could be filled with the ineffable more than any other thing. "Is it just pantomime?" the public asked. "Is it just shadow gestures?"

Despite the fact that Gertrude Stein and Alice B. had come before, the public asked a million stupid questions, written to the editor:

"Why do you like those rubber cocks but not 'real' cocks?"

"Why do you like those women walking down the street with dicks tucked in their boxer shorts?"

"Why do you like the ones in vintage shirts with 'Del' scrolled on the pocket?"

"Why do you like those odd ones who can't check a census box?"

"And what does that make you?"

PEGGY MUNSON

I told them all a parable.

I had a friend who was a cowboy. Cowboy always said, "Do not assume." The Cowboy said, "Assuming makes an ass of 'u' and 'me.'" Sometimes, when people looked between the cowboy's legs, they didn't see a horse. So then they were compelled to ask, "Are you a boy or girl?" The Cowboy found the question ludicrous. The Cowboy grinned and climbed onto the horse and said, "I am a cowboy. *Cowboy*'s what I am." The Cowboy didn't trifle with pedestrian concerns because pedestrians — of course — are forced to walk. The Cowboy wasn't keen on walking anywhere.

I saw the horses galloping between the legs of boys. They were stallions of a little girl's imagination, rescuers and friends and saints. America had taught me that the dick was everything. But then it gave me cowboys and a hundred lies of freedom. It gave me Annie Oakley and John Wayne. I knew a Wild West still existed on some plane. I went to find it in the borderland of boys. When a Cowboy walks — a bona fide one — you can see the horse between the Cowboy's legs. That's where I looked; that's where I saw. I saw what galloped like a sonnet over plains that never ended. Call it faith or fantasy or flesh, but I will call it how I liked to fuck. I liked to ride with those who were, in essence, born to ride.

And so the boys named Max or Blake or Jude or Ann showed up in well-worn jeans with just the right amount of slouch around their store-bought cocks. They passed through me like tourists at an airport, looking reunited or uncoupled when the lights flashed on. They never lied in inches, though they lied about their smoking habits or their jobs. But not in inches and for this, I had more luck than straight girls who wished they could hear the lies Gepetto heard and not the kind that shrunk. The lies of puny-headed boys could be rewritten with my pen.

"You will eat crow," some people said, but people

ORIGAMI STRIPTEASE

said that I would eat a lot of things: my words, my cock-iness, the gravel underneath my shoes. As far as I could see, I never ate enough. Besides, they couldn't say I was-n't good at what I did. I had a memory box of cocks, all widths and sizes, which these boys had fucked me with. I had the grace to make glass slippers fit. I had the coy-ness to dupe princes in the midnight hour. I had the hyperbolic glee to fill the paupers with deluded grandeur. It's not as if I never got attached. It's just—I knew I had to stay a pen-length back. Some boys I fucked were almost right for me. The one who slid her lips over my ass, and hands, her cock that hardened like a hunk of toffee on cold marble. The one who kissed like magnets fighting to deflect, then meeting metal. The one who lied, but knew her cock was honest. Some boys were almost right but all, in time, were farcical expressions fixed with spirit glue—just masks of faces haunting me.

I gave them more than my commitment could have given them. I made us three-dimensional with printer-planed and ballpoint-flattened words. I knew that paper language was the anthill of the human race—the thing that some of us woke up compelled to build upon, and others burned, so it could grow like once-charred prairie grass. Each time I slid beneath my desk to write, I did an origami striptease. First my paper stripped, and then the pen. And then, collapsed and naked, I imploded into both of them.

3.

But then the pens struck back. Perhaps they'd waited all their lives to lock me in an envelope.

I could not find the origins of "eating crow." But certainly, the more I talked about my own prodigious liberty, the more I felt like I was chewing birds. I munched on freedom, but it tasted awful as an oily wing. The thudding of the bodies on my high-thread-count, resistant bed began to wear at me. Most often, it is how inanimate and animate collide that causes accidents. It was like that with the pens and me. Pens caused me trouble. Pens made some call me "slanderer!" That said, it wasn't boys or hunger that destroyed me, no. It was The Sludge who ruined my life.

The sky had grown preposterously dark. The night had tucked its stars beneath a quilt of sorghum fields. The moon had scurried off as if it hid inside a nursery rhyme. I wore a swingy skirt. I put my hair in Pippi braids. I strolled downtown to hear a rock show hyped in *Spanky Smacky Spam*. I'd heard a lot of buzz about the band with the rambunctious post-punk name. While wandering through the borderlands, in fact, I pulled their poster down and rolled it in my armpit. *Come See The Sludge and Brother Zero!* barked the psychedelic font. I wasn't usually so obedient to advertising.

The place was packed. The crowd hummed like a cage from a mosquito breeding center. I nudged my way up to the bar and bought a beer, then found a place within the herd. A weaselly roadie tuned the bass and set the amps. A hush fell as the band took stage. The drummer started tapping out a beat, and suddenly the evening felt so intimate I had an urge to flee the room.

But something kept me there. The Sludge and Brother Zero played a song about a character named Jack that later seemed prophetic. To this day, I don't know

ORIGAMI STRIPTEASE

how The Sludge intuited those words. The mournful, mesmerizing tone was throbbing through my groin and turning me unwittingly into a groupie. I could not stop gazing at The Sludge. I stared insanely at his face, which wasn't dreamy but was rough, the kind of face that probably had a glass or two embedded in it once. The Sludge strummed D and C and G upon his Rickenbacker, and he opened up his lips and sang:

> *It was a barbed wire day wrapped around his*
> * temples but all Jack did was run.*
> *The street was a sentence that had sentenced*
> * him but all Jack did was run.*
> *He rode that street to the dirty end and all Jack*
> * did was run.*
> *Her body lay like a telegram saying urgent, stop,*
> * don't run.*
>
> *But all Jack did was run.*
> *All Jack did was run.*

His voice was beautiful and ugly all at once, like crystal water pouring from a gargoyle's mouth. I can't say when it was, the moment that he noticed me. After the band's set ended, I had found a vacant seat. The quarter of a beer I drank could not explain the heady feeling that had overtaken me. The Sludge was angled up against the bar. His hands were lobster-like; he moved like he was wearing armor plates. I forced myself to look away from him but heard the sound of leather bending as he sat beside my chair. His presence was magnetic. Girls were fluttering around his arms and touching his tattoos. I later learned The Sludge was never caught, no matter what he did to fuck up people's lives. He knew (the ones who know just know) that I preferred it rough. He grabbed me by my hair and yanked me back behind the bar.

"C'mon, unholy child," he snarled.

I did exactly what he said. The alley was a hundred colors nullified. He wore a military belt that wasn't full of bullets, but of pens. He pinched my nipples and he pressed his cock into my pubic bone. He shoved me to my knees and held my chin within one claw-like hand. "I know that you're the writer," he said gruffly. Then he stroked his cock and grabbed his belt. He glanced around to see if there were storm clouds stalking him. There were.

"I am," I said, and broke into a speedy smile.

I was impressed The Sludge knew who I was, as he had come from out of town. I had forgotten that a supervillain always knows his enemy. His dominance was thrilling me so much I felt like I was pooling on the ground and I should scoop myself into my normal outline, get a grip.

Our sexy vibe had changed the landscape utterly. I looked down at the ground and noticed that the night was made of ink. I glanced up and the squid-like blobs of people ambled past the gap between the buildings where the vantage lines collapsed. The sky was slick with ink, the kind of blackened soup that coats the wings of preternatural clouds. The buildings were all shadow, not a single cigar glow. It looked like something awful and disturbed inside a killer's brain—the Rorschach this and Rorschach that. The ink was chilling, and it drowned my organs in their beds. My body started shaking, but The Sludge smiled sloppily, as if the ink around his cartoon mouth had run.

"Think I could bum your jacket for a minute?" I asked sweetly. I was cold down to my kidneys.

"Did you pipe up?" he said. "Are you demanding things? Did you forget the magic 'pleeeease'? Do you need somebody to make you eat your words?"

I thought that he was being playful then, because he smirked. But no, his face turned serious, and then morose. He shoved his bulge against my lips so that I felt its diamond hardness on my teeth.

"No, Sir," I answered quickly.

I opened up my mouth and readied for his dick. I spread my throat. But then, just when I thought I'd blow his cock he made me suck his ballpoint pens. He broke the ends off with a snap, and stuck them one by one between my lips. And "suck" he ordered me. "That's right, suck back your words." That night of beaten raven tails, he made my lips and throat turn black and blue. He mocked: "Your writing is a column yard of *lies*. It's pap. You are not *news*." He slapped the news off of my face and made me swallow ink, the black and blue, like I was eating crow. The doctors said it caused what happened next, my body's dissolution. They said the causal agent must have been the poison of the ink. But also—this part was just me—my body filled with awful birds of my own making. The Sludge had filled me both with poison and with doubt.

The Sludge ran off. I crouched there coughing up the ink. If anything was not eclipsed by then—the moon, the stars, the lamps—it was eclipsed when I began my coughing fit. I must have been there hacking for an hour. Nobody stopped. The cabdriver who finally picked me up and drove me home talked on and on about Black Lung. "You've got the miner's lung," he said to me. "You'd better run to a physician." Then he told me how his brother had it, and his cousin Roger. "Moles," he said of them. "We are all moles where I come from—we're either mining coal or spying underground."

"Where do you come from? West Virginia?"

"No," he said, and gave a shifty glance. "A deeper South, with even wackier tobacco."

We reached the tunnel, and we drove under the bay. The tunnel was the place where everyone got quiet. We knew our voices—our vibrations—might collapse the earth around us. So we passed there with the superstitions about noise and silence we were taught. The cab-driver had squinted shut his eyes and gripped his hairy fingers on the wheel. He tilted back his head and rolled his foil coin eyelids toward the roof. He started chattering about the tunnels and the spies. He seemed unduly paranoid about the underworld.

"Please look out, sir," I tried to say. "This tunnel swallows cars for breakfast."

My voice came out a raspy sound, a sound of ink pens used to scratch a note in wood. The driver kept his head back and he drove with just his hands. I could not see much anyway—the road, his hands, his face—but still, I knew he wasn't driving with his eyes. I listened for the sound of something crashing but it never came.

We slid into the squint. The dawn was fingering the edges of the river. "The gophers burrowing through Eden will make all the city walls collapse," the cabdriver continued. "You are one, aren't you? Mole or spy? You like to live beneath?"

"Not me," I tried to say. The words came out inaudible. The ink had made it hard for me to speak.

"That's how it starts," he said, and shook his head. "The 'mutening.'"

"The what? The mutiny?" I tried to say. I was confused. "What ship?"

"The '*mute*ning,'" he said again. "The 'mutening' that starts the miner's lung."

I shook my head to let him know I didn't understand.

"Like 'deafening,'" he said, impatiently. "With mute. That's how it starts. Like deafening with mute. Soon you will flounder through a spell of stagnant time until your squeaky speech is obsolete."

He parked the cab and helped me walk up to my stoop. I gave him twenty dollars that he took with hairy knuckles. Somehow I got into my bed and slept. The morning sun put gilding over everything. I pulled the drapes.

ORIGAMI STRIPTEASE

I woke up later spitting vitriol and feeling very ill. The day was pouring through the curtains and my body ached. My lymph nodes hurt. My throat felt blocked, as if it were a jammed but anxious gun. My mouth bled ink. I tried to read a book, but words were blurred and danced around the page, as if the ink no longer had parameters. The slightest movement made me nauseous. Standing wore me out. But worst of all, I had to wait within the days until they let me leave my house, or play, or fuck. Most days, my brain felt muddied by the injury The Sludge had left. I could not think of words to write. A blush washed all the black and blue away, but still, I felt the rustle and the hunger of the crows. The noises all around me were acute and hurt my brain—a kettle whistling or a pickup roaring by outside. All sounds were amplified. I heard the cabdriver's voice inside my head and knew then what he meant. The world grew deafening the more I was becoming mute.

The naysayers were right: I ate a murder full of crows. I crunched the bones between my teeth in hopes that they would calcify my will to overcome, in hopes that they would grow me bones and wings. I closed my shutters, and I let the steam from soup occlude my days. I didn't think of boys or cocks. I hadn't yet met Jack.

4.

I was ungodly ill for months that later turned to years.

My walls were made of rice paper. They were too thin, and noise could scatter everywhere. My bones were made of cardboard tubes. So, when I slept, they folded under me, and when I woke, my limbs were bent in odd configurations. I hurt from how the cold blew through my walls and through my skin. I learned how barriers — the one that keeps the blood from brain with certain molecules, the one that keeps the boys from girls with certain chromosomes — are only strips of paper. Small vibrating strips of paper trying to make a sound — the architecture of kazoos. My walls unfolded neatly into diorama boxes. It should have been an easy coup to rip my way out of my paper room. But I could not. I was a writer. My bones were made of paper. If I ripped that exoskeleton, I ripped my own.

I could write about the vomiting and vertigo, the migraines and the fireballs in my throat. Or I could talk about the way I read *The Plague* repeatedly and thought there must be other people hiding in their darkened rooms and puking and unraveling. Or I could talk about the times I tried to breach the sunlight and I found myself so lost I had to pull over and slump over the steering wheel and rest and catch my breath. Reluctantly, I always turned around and drove back home, defeated by the smallest distances. And yes, I could say how I passed out in the shower, woke up hunched into a ball of bruises on the ground. But these details, if they're anything, are only here to emphasize the ways that pens destroyed and pens redeemed. The way that pens were given, pens were lost. The way my safety ended when I smashed into an inkwell of internal bruising. No eloquence, no naked pens, could show the small crimped ribs of that.

ORIGAMI STRIPTEASE

Besides, I had a lot of problems superceding explanation of my plight.

"Get out, get out!" I screamed at nothing in particular, and waved my fevered arms. In my delirium, it seemed my house was full of snakes. I tried to keep the snakes out of my passageways. They crawled into my mouth and slithered out. They spilled out into macramé around my lips. They tried to climb into my nostrils, and they tried to go inside my ears. They tumbled in and out of knots. Some days, my house was full of charging rhinos. I lay down upon the floor and all of them, all forty or a hundred, trampled over me. They ran through walls the way that football players charge through paper spheres before a game. The drafts blew in until I patched the holes. That is, if I could peel the flattened paper of my body from the floor.

Some days were like stigmata. On the calendar, they bled.

Some days I could not grab the phone. It was a Bering Strait away.

On good days, I sat out and watched the skateboards rattling by. Those days were so miraculous. I crammed my unwashed hair into a hat and sipped on herbal tea. "Hey punks!" I yelled at skateboard boys who thought I was an apparition. The neighbors, when they passed, all claimed that I looked wonderful. Ironically, the illness — though it inked me up inside — acted inversely on the outside — pulled my skin back from my luster, so I glowed.

At night, I couldn't sleep.

My alpha sleep became a wolf and bit my delta sleep to shreds. I slept a Dead Sea sleep in which I couldn't sink because of all the salt. My knees felt like old chicken bones pulled from the trash. My body sunk away until I got so thin my bones ran into everything. I threw the covers off and pulled them on. I tried a dozen medications. Finally, I took to staying up at night and sleeping fitfully throughout the days. At night, I sensed the other bodies sleeping in closed houses all around me like a smooth collective lake. I felt them near me, just as one can feel a lake nearby from how mosquitoes talk to one another, or the grass just seems to bend over a bank and drink. I slept a wartime blackout sleep, as if an arsenal of bombs slept under me.

I could say I never thought of fucking, but I always thought of it. I thought about it all the time since I was always lying down. I touched myself as if I were a light switch that would not turn on, but I could not conceive of flashlights or of candles. I could not imagine blackouts or a world before the lightbulb was invented. Suddenly, I found my body fascinating. While I had left it up to others—boys—to pleasure me before, I now was like a rich kid thrown into a shack with nothing but a ragged blanket and a set of hands. "I'm building character," I thought at first. "I am unfettered now." I masturbated in a weird delirium, reduced to conversations between nerves.

One day, I finally had the strength to leave my house. I'd driven by the pastures and the barns. I'd driven by the borderlands. I went to Hornet's Baggage Claim to find my bag. I had the sense that everything I owned was lost. I had an impulse—spawned from feverish delusion— that my life could be restored if I just found my bag and reconstructed what was in it, even though there never was a bag. My trip was subterranean, a tour of war tunnels beneath the surface noise.

The Claim—as it was sometimes called—was where the lost bags went. The ones that should have been in Mexico, or Prague, or Iowa, but never made their flight. The airlines sent them there. It was a thrift store for the orphan goods nobody claimed. For goods a businessman was red-faced over, screaming at an airline girl in Prague.

ORIGAMI STRIPTEASE

I pulled the jingling door. I ran my fingers over silky dresses that had never made their dates. That's when I spotted Jack. He paced beside the aisle of cowboy boots. I might have thought that he was just a teenage guy, except for how his hands caressed the snakeskin and the ostrich hide. I wanted them, his hands, to pull my head out of the sand. In fact, he touched me by the pull of his indifference, the way stones do.

Jack glanced around the store for help. The inventory, like the bags, was half-unpacked as if it never really had a home. "Which ones came from a crash?" Jack asked the single worker there. His hands were moving over everything. He liked the texture of the ostrich skin.

"The grab bags," she said, pointing to a table full of bags that were sealed shut. "We charge ten bucks for both the bag and all the junk inside."

She fiddled with her price gun. She was trying to figure out if she should flirt. She looked down at her manicure, then up at Jack. Jack stared unblinking at the woman's face. I'd been to Hornet's many times. The owner might as well have been a mannequin. His name was Bob Rialdo, and he never moved. I used to walk right by him in the store and think he wasn't real.

"Doesn't the FAA take those away?" asked Jack. He seemed surprised that she had answered perfunctorily and with no trace of shock.

"Not if they're unclaimed and there's no investigation. Not if it is just another traveler." She pushed her bangs back from her eyes.

"Then I'll take this one here."

The bag he picked was mutty-looking and well-traveled. He peeled out bills but he had only nine. I heard the cashier counting them. His cheeks grew flushed as he was digging through his pocket for more change. I couldn't stand to watch him struggle while she tapped her garish nails and flashed a flirty smile. She grew annoyed as he fished for the final bill. I walked up by his bent, shaved head.

"I'll cover ten percent," I said, and shoved a dollar in Jack's face.

"You're on," said Jack. "But I won't be your charity. You get a cut." He didn't look at me, but I was glad for this. I felt the red jump from his face to mine. The cashier saw it clearly, how I wanted Jack.

That's how I got the naked pen, the Tip 'n' Strip that Jack had found within a pile of boxer shorts. Jack also gave me ten percent of all the rest, our cache of crashed belongings. The bag contained: a water gun, a squirting flower, condoms, boxers, trousers, ties, a plastic rose, a wrinkled photograph of lovers, one long vibrator, a pad of paper, and the naked pen. That was before I knew how much Jack *was* an unclaimed bag, how much I *was* a single-engine Cessna down. How much his place inside of me gave balance and his absence made me bank away from every destination. Then we walked together through the lot. Jack swung the bag. I tipped and stripped the pen. We leaned against our cars and didn't speak. The wind was blowing everything around. Trash dervishes whirled crazily around the corner of the store. Jack swung his hand the way the wind might blow a swing. He caught my hand in his and pulled me toward his lips.

The first time it was just a kiss. A gentle kiss between our cars.

Jack's leather pressed against my chest, and both of us could barely stand. We leaned together like a saw-horse, holding one another up. From being out and walking, I was sick and wobbling like a drunk, and Jack was too—though I did not know he was sick right then. He kissed the way that children whisper, with a kind of intimate regret. Like he had told me awful secrets in that kiss. Jack pressed me up against the windows of the car and kissed me while he held my neck. That's where I found exactly what I wanted, at the map point where all lost things went. His lips were perfect, and his palms moved down my arcing back. The dead letters of never-spilled confessions spilled between our hands.

"You've got the saddest smoked-out eyes," said Jack. "You've got the prettiest charred hair."

The temporality of our encounter should have been so clear, but I could not believe it then. The clouds were moving in the way they only do in flatlands, where the sky can barely hold its body up. The barometric pressure there was palpable, with sudden drops that nearly made a person's heart collapse. The air grew eerie sometimes, as it paused and built inside its whistle tube. Jack leaned against his hood and put his forehead in his hands. He looked like he might wilt. "What's wrong?" I asked. He squinted at the sky and straightened up. "I'm fine," Jack said. "Just flushed. I'll call you later, yes?" I saw it for a moment, Jack's ill health.

The doctors had told Jack:

"You'll live."

"You'll die."

"It's nothing."

"It's unclear."

"What gender should I check here, boy? Or girl?"

A dozen viruses could permeate the heart and mind, and some of them could shuttle mercury or ink or atrazine. The blood-brain barrier and pericardium were not as ironclad as they claimed. Jack hinted that his fascination with crashed luggage had to do with why he was so sick. He told me that an aerobatics pilot had flown him to corkscrew in the sky. That day, he claimed, the engine stalled. Jack hit his head and almost died and broke the autonomic parts of things. The broken wiring in his brain made him malfunction too, his vagus nerve, his walk, his panic-stricken eyes. This left him frozen in the walleyed headlights way too many times. I knew these stories were all lies. His doctors called him sick, diseased, and ill—not injured—or they didn't call at all.

PEGGY MUNSON

I think he liked the grandiosity of saying he'd been etching in the sky. Somebody told me that he'd had rheumatic fever. Someone said cancer and then liver problems and then AIDS. Jack probably bought his story for ten dollars. But at least he didn't lie in inches. No, Jack fibbed to make his peace with temporality and truth.

5.

It took a week for him to call. " I need to see the pen," the voice said on the other end. "She's my pneumatic tube to you. I need to see her so she'll write you that I want to see you too."

Much later, I learned this: Jack always used these words with caution, *want* and *need*. "I'm busy, but she'll take a message," I said coyly on the other end. I held the girlie pen and started writing on a scratch pad. "Jack!" I wrote. I underlined his name. I doodled pictures in the margins: people fucking, girls undressing, smut.

"Tell her to tell you this. I sense an imminence," said Jack. "As if there is a fuse between my eyes and I am watching it. I'm going to blow."

"The borderland boys know my house," I said. "Just ask them where I live."

Soon after that, the snarling panting thing came rapping at the door. Not Jack, but love.

We both adopted it. We *knew* it was a beast. I hadn't been in love before, but still I knew. The line between an incubus and lover — when one's never been in love — is slight. They both attack you in your sleep. They both invade. They both disrupt.

But still, I let it in.

The first era was one of fire. We put the mettle to the kettle. Then, after the weeks Jack made me wait, we thought we could control our sex drive, but we couldn't. We were snagged. He threw me on the mattress that suddenly felt as big as fields of sheep. We started carefully, our breath controlled as bagpipes, and then everything unwinding like a riot. "I want to Kama Sutra every goddamn inch of you," said Jack, as he was ripping off my underwear and turning me into a hyperbolic pretzel on

43

his fingertips. He was a careless surveyor so tangled in coordinates he yelped when he got lost inside my pussy. We tried to think of other things to do, but once he finally touched me, we broke out with heat. Our lives were scorched. The sun became a weed that littered every field with dandelion yellow, while the flowers and their prettied sexuality shirked off. Jack fucked the way a kid swings in a swing when he has ten minutes until the end of recess and he really thinks that he can kick the clouds. Jack didn't come inside of me but kicked upstream into the mackerel sky, and we *believed* his dick had cum: that was enough.

"Come on," I moaned, and squeezed him tight between my legs. "Why don't you give me every drop?"

So maybe we believed too much. We weren't confined by the parameters of what a body was expected to provide. I wasn't sure if I could differentiate between the viscera and their imposters.

I tried to stop.

I held the pen over my chest, much like a hari-kari knife. I tried to generate new stories for The Cherry Vault. I fought to keep my literary distance. Then the doorbell interrupted me, and it was easy to ignore my paper caricatures in favor of the flesh. When I unhooked the lock, Jack put his hand over my mouth and pushed me in the house. "You hoggish little paper smut machine," he snarled into my ear. "Are you alone?"

I nodded.

"Good," he said.

He clamped his hands over my eyes and held me up at fingerpoint as he directed me into another room. "March, prisoner," he ordered me.

I heard a snap and clinking sound. He gripped my skull as he positioned me against the wall. I heard the whirring of the pulled-out belt, which sounded like those metal tops controlled by string. I caught my breath and steadied up against the wall while Jack became the orange aura of a woodstove, warming me with all of his unmoving heat.

"I think that maybe we should sto—," I tried to say.

Then suddenly, a *whap*. He started chanting with his belt. He hit my ass and thighs and skin, *thwap, thud*. The air was humming past the leather with a symphony of singing bowls. My skin turned into coals and then he came down with his kisses, balm for all the burns.

" —Should *stop*," I said.

I tried to put up barriers, but he would not allow it. *Whap*, the belt came down and hit the welts on top of welts on top of ass.

"Goddammit, give yourself to me," demanded Jack.

He took my wrists and spun me into him, then kissed me then he threw me to the floor. "Oh man, I've got to get inside of you."

His rubber balls jerked automatically, like venom sacs. He slid his palms over my nipples, and he traced his finger on my lip. There was a red moon calling him behind my tongue and teeth. There was a sanguine sailor's moon.

"Hey little Cosmonaut," I told the cock, as I moved down, my wet tongue teasing it. "I've got the moon inside, the moon."

I pulled him in with all my gravity. My knees were pressed into the cold wood floors. I slid my lips down on his cock. He moaned and pushed his way into my throat—"Go on and suck it, take it in." He clawed my hair. "Go on and work your pretty lips."

He ripped my panties off while I was sucking on his dick. He ran one gloved hand over my cunt. I knew that I was dripping.

"See how you're melting on my hand?" he asked.

I didn't want to melt. I didn't want to worry over Icarus and his waxed wings. I didn't want to crash into the earth like everyone who tried to fly with a flimsy home invention.

But everything, with Jack and me, went through a thousand cycles in a day—both hot and cold. Just when I tried to hold him under a magnifying glass, the world around us broke up into rice and paper circles. All around us were a million paper dots. And we were there, a pointillist creation on a canvas blank with possibility. I wanted him to break me into parts. "Come on," I begged. "Just shatter me down to my molecules, down to the smallest bits."

"How far?" asked Jack, and slid his cock inside of me. "How many bits?"

"Just fuck me with a sledgehammer on windshield glass."

Then later, I was lying on my stomach with my face pressed into fluff. I smelled the dust of our last weeks. My wrists were tied. My ankles were spread out and strapped to corners of the bed. Jack left me prone and went to read a magazine.

He breathed behind me, and he traced my outline with one finger, then he slid one finger into me.

I begged for more, a salutary handshake, something, anything besides a little bit.

"You never get enough," he scolded, spanking me. He pulled back, threateningly, as if he'd really leave.

"Jack, please."

"You want to go to war? You want a protest song?"

I begged for it.

Jack slowly slid his whole fist into me.

Next there were lazy days, days when we couldn't push outside of illness to make love. The wrecking ball that slept beside me in my bed made me distrust my own unruly flesh. We laid back, and we watched the days uncoil. Jack wove his fingers through my fingers: "Look, we made a rattan trivet out of hands," he said. We fixed our eyes upon the naked pen. I thought that our monastic style of entertainment had the markings of true love. "Make her undress again," said Jack.

We propped ourselves against my pillows, and I tipped her up so that her pinup dress began to disappear, then tipped her down. Our sickness had a way of making time distort. The hours seemed bent around a spoon. "The Zen of naked pens," claimed Jack. "That's our religion here."

He took a finger, and he traced the seahorse shapes of both my ears. These simple things, though so mundane to others, were infused with surface tension that would break when we next fucked. We felt the tingle of the tension, even then.

The weeks spent convalescing would have tortured us in isolation, but they weren't so terrible in tandem. Late at night, I mopped his brow and wrung the sweat out of his T-shirts, and he steadied me as I walked lilting to the kitchen to get crackers. In the days, we ate the way that soldiers eat—from jars and cans, utilitarian. I found it too exhausting even picking up a spoon. My heart let out a shrunken rattle, like a seed inside a gourd. My brain could barely hold a thought: it was a butterfly net and my words were gnats. Jack grew as skinny as a railroad tie. I fed him jerky from a bag. He pulled a blanket to my chin, although my body—wracked with chills— could not warm up. He wrapped me up in him. I rolled him up in me.

Jack cuddled me against his chest. I coughed into my fist. I felt like ink was rising up inside of me, a wave of ink, until I choked it down. "I'm tortured by that night," I said. Jack knew about The Sludge, the poisoning, the way I went along with it. "It was like everything I had created coming back to try and kill me, as a child would pull a knife against a parent. Ink, the irony of ink."

"We've chewed our alibis and courtroom sketches, haven't we? I know I have, I've eaten ink," said Jack, his voice all quiet.

"What do you mean?" I asked.

"I mean, there is a lot that you don't know," said Jack.

I started seeing what Jack meant. He meant that he saw afterimages. Just stare too long at printed words, then pull them from your sight: slight shadows stay fixed on your retina, then fade away. The shadows are decrepit ruins, Old Panama, not shelter from your commonest hallucinations but a haunting space. The strange remains abandon you inside the ruins of your own brain, and every brain connects the lines and dots of broken things in different ways. I started seeing what he meant: our damage severed us.

On days that we were well enough to drive, Jack often took me to watch silent movies on a barn then fucked me on a blanket in his pickup truck.

In late July, it wasn't ever cold. It was the kind of night when ice cream parlors kept their doors agape past sunset hours. With all the tinkering on literal egress in daytime, night was for ineffable concerns and ice cream cones. Each couple sprawled upon the grass and talked for hours about the paranormal. Crickets tuned their legs at ten. The highways were seductive serpents, hot with sun that turned the water from each errant hose to steam. We laughed like horny teenagers and rolled around. Jack struggled with my bra. He tried to get it open with one hand. We saw the lights of cars reflecting on the side mirrors and kept our heads bowed as we kissed against the yellow steel.

There was a lone tree that had grown beside that field for fifty years.

Jack pulled back suddenly, his eyes as wide as cannon shot. I turned to see what he was looking at and saw the remnants of a broken swing that made an eerie tempo in the warm, adagio night breeze. The broken swing was hanging from a jutting branch. It only had a rope attached to its left side and not its right. The wooden board was knotted to the rope, a crooked thing that made an awful *crreeeeeak*. The swing was suddenly in motion, swaying like a windsock, and Jack curled his body up in terror.

"No," he said. "I can't see that right now. Not that."

"What do you see?" I asked. "What is it, Jack?" I only saw suggestion and asymmetry. The swing implied that children, who had gotten splinters in their asses, grew up without bothering to rebalance the past. But why was that so awful?

"I see a game of hangman with the moon," said Jack. He hugged his knees against his chest.

"What's that?" I asked. "What's hangman with the moon?"

"I cannot tell you that."

I think Jack summoned up the lightning then. It started in the sky, communicating cloud to cloud to break the heat. The lightning fingered out and acid-etched the fields with light. We sat up, startled, then we watched it roll across the sky. Jack gripped my clammy hand. My bra was hanging halfway off, and I felt slutty and remorseful, so I pulled Jack's jacket over me. The lightning was a distant pyrotechnic show. Then sudden-ly — as if it had seduced us through a lulling script until it reached a climax — it licked down and struck the tree. It made a violent jagged burst and then a crackle that split both our eardrums open, and the lightning cleaved the trunk into a large piece and a smaller chunk that fell away. The light tricked everything: I saw a jagged line long after it was gone, as if my eyes were simply tintype, taking it. My heart was beating wildly from the boom. The piece of tree that held the swing began to topple with an exhalation of its char and smoke. Jack squeezed my hand like he was watching an assassination.

"Let's seek cover in the barn or truck," I said. "We're sitting ducks right here."

"The barn," said Jack. He could not take his eyes off of the tree. "Go in, I'll meet you in a second."

Then he pulled his work gloves on. I looked over my shoulder as he shuffled toward the tree and lifted up a corner of the swing to pull the dangling broken section from the tree, then heaved it in the pickup truck. Once safe inside the barn, Jack seemed relieved. He wiped the black off on his jeans.

"I know this sounds ridiculous," he said. "But what I saw was not a swing."

"What was it then?"

"It was a boy with rock-star hair. A guy I knew who died."

My eyes felt strange, askew, as if I saw him through a wobbly bit of antique glass. Lightning leaves an afterimage too, that jagged line behind the eyelid when you stare right at the flash. Jack laid me on the straw and pulled a blanket over me. He stroked his bulge. He gripped my hand and rubbed it on the dick that slid out sideways down his leg.

"I want my girl to jerk me off," he said.

I was not fully present in my skin, but I obliged. My absence didn't seem significant. No more than one whore's early tricks seem meaningful when she has turned a hundred more.

Perhaps my motives should have been examined, but they weren't.

I stroked his cock to make the night erase. I told myself I was the master of reality. That I could make it disappear beneath the rubber pink. Time pivoted upon that moment, as it pivots on a lie. I made a conscious turn toward myth. I would regret it. People always do. But in the heat it seemed innocuous, or more: an act of love. I saw that Jack was tangled in his past. I wanted to extract him from his snarl. He was relaxing as I rubbed his cock, and I was glad to help him leave his haunting thoughts. I had become a part of someone's fraying tapestry. I pulled his string. I got my trigger finger ready. This is how a love affair creates a dictator and a Manchurian candidate. I tried to turn into his pain's assassin then.

"Is this the way you like?" I asked, my eyes aglow.

I saw my eyes from far away, how they were sitting in an ashtray of dead stars.

"Speed up," Jack said.

And then he somehow brought me back. He slid the bottom of my skirt up to my thigh, then eased one palm beneath the hem. Oh God, how I was dying for that hand. He creased my panties so they split my pussy lips. He ran his finger up and down until he felt with certainty that I was wet, that I was drained of reason, spilling out. He clasped my hand and put it on a saddlehorn behind my head. "Just hold on till the cows come home," he said, and pried my legs apart until my skirt fanned out. The storm the lightning ushered in was pouring now, the kind of rain that seems militaristic, how aggressively yet orderly it falls. It hammered on the outside of the barn, and there were leaks, but not near us, just background taps. He looked around for something sharp but all he found were hedge trimmers.

"Keep still." He pulled my panties out and snipped them off.

And then, the chaos of the fight began. The friend or foe debate. The clouds were loosening all over, and the night grew bilious and uncontained. I knew exactly how implosion happened since I loved to watch the shows about tornadoes. Here, the barn would fall the way a single-storied card house falls, exposing everything at once. And that's how I fell too. I shed my sheaf, and I was nothing but the passion and the glint inside. I wrapped my arms around his back to get him deeper into me, to hold him in. I loved it that he couldn't run away, that rain had formed a wall.

But Jack would run. Jack always ran. That night had spooked my boy, and he would flee from me. For me, it was the opposite. He was so burned against my retina I couldn't ever see another boy the way that I saw him, no matter how he turned the hot to cold or fled from me.

"That's it," I said, and hugged him close. "Stay deep inside of me."

6.

The next era was one of push and pull. Each time we got too close, he ran away and didn't call, and then came back. I hated it. I wondered what was wrong with me, why he would leave. I thought there must be things in me that made him run.

I knew that he was wounded, but I didn't think that that was why. No, it must have been something unspeakable in me.

Jack talked about the things that happened to him, but in intimation. I got the sense that some abomination had occurred, some act of which he could not speak. The days together were contented — warm and sluggish afternoons in which our bodies met like octopus and fishnet. The nights that he slept over in my bed, he whistled from his nose. He twitched erratically and woke up yelling. He sleepwalked, and one time I found him in the other room, where he had filled two bowls with ice and put his hands in, even though he was asleep.

I reached out and I grabbed the ice, but then he woke. He started screaming.

"Jack, what is it?"

"Nothing," he said, owl-eyed. "Go to sleep."

Another night, I found him lying in a bathtub full of ice. His lips were plum, his cheeks a bluish blush. I screeched and flipped the lights on.

"Jack!" I screamed. I shook him so the ice rattled against the tub.

He woke and said, "I'm freezing. Where's my spooky?" Spooky's what he called his childhood blanket — fleecy white, a friendly ghost of cloth.

I dug him out with just my hands. I pulled the ice away and threw it on the floor. I grabbed his frozen-turkey flesh and yanked him out and wrapped him up in towels and rubbed his body down.

"What is it, Jack? Please talk to me." I begged.

"Remember how you used to make me drinks?" he asked. "Well this is mine — somnambulism on the rocks." He forced a weary smile.

The next time that I heard the crackle of the ice-cube tray, I yelled, "You're dead, Jack, dead. Just stop."

Each time I heard the sound, I had the same Pavlovian response. It was a galling chiropractic sound that shocked my eyes awake. I took to sleeping with my shoes beside my bed. One night he filled a kiddy swimming pool with bags of ice. I ran into the yard and caught him emptying the bags. He never seemed surprised by how much ice he had or how much cold his body could sustain. I tried to act like it did not affect me when I paid the tab at the convenience store and caught him leering at the freezer bags. I tried to hide my anger when I found him on the Internet, surveying every sleek refrigerator with an ice machine. I thought that his obsession would just melt away, but I was wrong. One night I walked out in the yard and tripped over Jack's shovel. The lawn was vapory and all I knew was that the right side of the bed had emptied while I slept. I stumbled through the grass until I saw what he had done. He'd dug a shallow grave and left a pile of dirt. He'd filled the makeshift grave with ice. He lay atop the ice, curled up in pj's, sleeping like a child.

I told myself that he was not self-mutilating. I hadn't found Mercator lines on wrists. The ice could symbolize a means of preservation. Besides, he wasn't running any more. In fact, he hardly ever left my house. I knew some nights he had come back from doing it. He crawled into the bed, and suddenly, I woke up shivering. He rolled his body toward me, and his hands felt cold as grapes. One night, when he was opening the freezer door, I shook him from his grog and asked him what had happened, what the world had done to him. I said to him,

ORIGAMI STRIPTEASE

"Was it your family, Jack? Did they do something? Was it them?"

This question made him violent. He grabbed a fist of cubes and threw them to the wall. "I have been traitorous enough to them," he said defensively. "Some people sit beside a frozen devil, live with anger in their hearts, and that's how they are born. Don't you know children, even children, can be wrong? So no, do not blame Mom and Dad." He grabbed my sleeve, confused. He started madly flinging ice against the walls. And after that, I had to lock him in the bedroom, hide the key. Some nights I heard him crashing around the room.

"Why don't you let me sleep?" he yelled and grew combative when I tried to shake his eyes awake. "Why don't you ever let me sleep?"

It's true he only slept contentedly when packed in ice, a mortal carcass, trapped in hypothermic peace. Otherwise, he tossed around in nightmares all night long, and I could give him nothing, not a bit of solace then.

The days had shifted imperceptibly once Jack could not find ice. He wouldn't touch me when we went to sleep, and I felt cold beside him, frozen off. One day, a vintage truck appeared across the street, with shiny finished walnut on the sides. In script, it said, *McCusker's Ice Refrigeration*. The letters had been freshly painted, but the truck flank was a palimpsest, with years of writing rubbed down underneath the logo. I couldn't see a driver sitting in the seat. I paced around it checking, looking for antennae, listening for the hum of monitors or radio transmission. Jack would not mention that the truck was always there, though it was oddball and anachronistic. He acted like it didn't bother him but drew the shades and wouldn't go outside. "There's no respectable reality on television," he said while wildly flipping channels. The truck was parked across the street all day and night.

PEGGY MUNSON

Those nights, Jack huddled carefully against the edge of the mattress, and he didn't leave. He left a kidney bean impression on the sheets.

The next five days, I walked around the truck. I tried to catch somebody in the act of spying or loitering. I hid behind a bush and waited, or I watched it from my car a block away. I couldn't stand that Jack and I pretended it was nothing. "You have to tell me, Jack," I finally said, and cornered him. "What is this all about?"

"What's what about?"

"That truck."

"You mean the ice truck? It's what people in the olden days would use to fill their iceboxes."

"I know that much. But you don't think it's strange that it appeared when you were freezing your balls off and — probably — your chains with ice?"

"I never think about ice when I'm not asleep," Jack lied. I knew his game. I saw the longing looks he gave each time we passed a freezer aisle.

"But, Jack," I asked, and drew a breath. "Has some-one come for you?" His face got white.

Jack wouldn't say another thing. At ten the morning after that, I stormed up to the truck. It was the gesture of a codependent Pollyanna and I knew it, but I planned to sleuth my way into Jack's heart. A wizened little man was sitting in the driver's seat. He wore tweed pants, tweed cap, an ironed linen shirt. His shoes were shined. His head was just a little pustule, and his hair was white and frizzed around his face in the humidity. I faced the codger's side. He looked off in the distance, and he chewed his teeth. I knew he thought it rude that I was staring.

"You have to go," I said to him. I said it sternly so he'd know that I meant business. "You've got to take this truck away."

"I can't do that," he said. "Nope, missy, no-sir-ee." His neck was stiff, stiff as a broom. His jaw was tight, and he was hunched, a squat jack-in-the-box packed in his little truck. He looked like he might come unsprung at any juncture.

"This is a farce," I barked, and madly swung against the truck. "Nobody has an icebox any more. What are you trying to pull?"

He cocked his head. "Is that what you're riled up about?" He broke into a little mocking smile. "Some kind of ploy involving ice?"

"Nobody has an icebox here."

"Dry ice," he said, triumphantly. "I've got dry ice in back."

"Dry ice?"

"This afternoon, I have to take a kidney to the city," he said. "A boy, I'm guessing seventeen, who's on dialysis. Or he will die."

"Why are you waiting here? Why don't you wait a little closer to the hospital?" I asked.

"I'm waiting for a kidney here," he said, as if it was the most banal of deeds.

As soon as he began to speak, I noticed that a dry-ice smoke was seeping from the truck. It wasn't true combustion smoke, but theater smoke tiptoeing around my ankles. It curled its filiform and puffy nimbus up and down the street. I got the sense that we were acting in a play, and if I didn't turn around and hurry home, the street would dissipate. But then, I felt a sudden sense of panic, thinking that the man had come to take a scalpel to my flesh. I held my hands against my lower back. The old man looked at me and laughed. I turned around and raced back home and slammed the door and panted fearfully and saw Jack sitting there. His runty sickly flesh looked weak and sacrificial.

"There's no respectable reality outside," I said. "Let's watch TV."

The next day, both the man and truck had gone. But they returned. And that time, when I told the man that he should leave, he said, "I can't. I'm waiting for a heart."

7.

"I need to know what's going on," I said.

"You've been too sick to go outside," said Jack. "That's all."

"Please Jack. I need to know."

"Just watch," said Jack. He pointed to the nightly news. "You'll see."

The TV filled up with Zamboni ice-resurfacing machines. There was a fugitive light peeking from the hall and nothing but the glowing box inside my room. The curtains were in shock, unmoving in the light or dark. I felt a spooky trill of notes go down my spine. The wooden truck seemed quaint compared to the Zambonis on TV. "You've been too sick to go outside," said Jack. He put his hand against my forehead. "Feel. You're burning up."

"But what are those Zambonis doing here?" I asked.

Jack shrugged. "We'll find out on the news," he said.

As hypnagogic weeks ensued, my fever climbed and capsized me, and we became addicted to the nightly news. We could not wait to turn it on. While I plunged into deep delirium, Zamboni ice-resurfacing machines had commandeered our town. They lined up at the edge as squat as bulldogs, and at dusk, they looked like mini-tanks pretending to be peacekeepers. At night, I heard their awful scraping sounds and thought they must be shaving down ice surfaces (but where?). By day, they stared directly at the downtown square. "Don't be alarmed," the mayor said. "They're just preparing for the new ice-skating rink." I peered behind the curtains and did not see cranes or concrete blocks. The ice-resurfacers were menacing. I entered into a police state of the mind. "Why are they here?" I asked, and grabbed for Jack.

"You've been too sick to go outside," he said again. "Calm down. Let me massage your back." Before he grabbed the oil, our eyes locked lovingly on the TV. The trailer for a special on Zamboni ice-resurfacing machines was on.

We could not turn it off.

In time, we talked in "we" instead of "you" or "I," as if we'd joined a club. The nightly news made us a part of outside life. It told us that our outer world was just as poisoned as our inner world. "The town is full of filth," the mayor said, his face washed out by TV lights. "This town is rotting out. And why? Our moral decency is at an all-time low. Our city center is in disrepair. The recreation club is nothing but necrotic tissue and its pestilence will spread to other buildings if we don't contain the filth." His speech grew more austere. "If things don't change, we might just have to flood the town, then freeze it off the surface of the map, and scrape it down again," he said. "We might just have to—" Then he paused, and took a breath. "Resurface everything." The cameras panned the ice-resurfacing machines, which looked like pit bulls—cute, but dangerous. I pulled the drapes and saw the TVs lighting up in every house.

The whole town seemed to watch the nightly news, to see if he would crack down on a given neighborhood, or if the ice-resurfacing machines had moved. But they did not. The news became a mere distraction, and its content changed. It used to show the tragedies and pleasantries of any city—freak electrocutions, drug busts, local landmarks burning down. It stood for local truth. But now it played an endless looping tape of the Zambonis with a sidebar on the recreation club's demise. The newscasts often interviewed one man who used to drive Zambonis, Buzz, a queer potato from a cabin at the edge of town, and we loved hearing Buzz. He was a stumpy eighty-five-year-old who had devoted all his working years to skating rinks. They liked to say he gave "the honest buzz" about the news, but then they laughed at him—that senile coot.

ORIGAMI STRIPTEASE

And there was one more thing. Jack couldn't get it up unless he watched the nightly news. I used to say the only thing worse than a flaccid child's balloon was someone who could not get wood with silicone, but Jack could not. "I need an anchor for myself," Jack said, defensively. "I need an anchorman. That's all." He gave a sullen shrug.

"Can't we try once without the television on?" I yanked him from the square of light. I grabbed the black remote and pushed the "off." I opened up the drawer that held his dick. Instead of Gideon's Bible there it was: its form wrapped in a straw-colored bandana. "Just this once?"

"Why can't we do it to the news?" he whined, and grumbled as he sidled to the bed. His dick looked like a strange, anachronistic toy: a stocking stuffer from the era of transistor radios. My camisole and T-shirt made a silky slither as they dropped. I slid beneath him, and I pulled him by the harness onto me. But Jack was hesitant. He grabbed the tube of aloe gel I used for lube. "I want to fuck you with my hand," he said. He started easing fingers into me, and then his fist. He kissed me, and he grabbed at me. He braced his other palm. I started opening. Then I looked up and noticed he was chipping at a piece of plaster on the wall. His fingertip had almost pried it off. "Goddammit, Jack!" I yelled. "You're thinking about walls."

"I'm not. I'm thinking about *you.*"

"Admit it, Jack. You want to watch the recreation club again," I said. "Well, fine. Just watch." I threw the black remote at him and stormed out of the room. I glanced around to see him fixed on the TV. His hand was moving up and down his cock.

That's when I knew we'd moved into a trance.

The first day I had watched the news, I saw the skeletal insides of where I'd once done figure eights on pompom-

ed skates: the recreation club. The club, once young and
fit, was now diseased. "It isn't mold," the mayor said.
"It's definitely not a patch of mold." At first they thought
it was a simple case of *Stachybotrys chartarum* but no, the
recreation club had grown necrosis in its walls. Our
trusted structure had corrupted from within. Some said
it was a toxic spider that had sneaked in through a toilet
pipe and bit the building in its atrium. Some pinned the
blame on South American bacteria. Some said the rec
club had been stricken when a band of llamas pranced
by it the week the spinners passed through town, and
rubbed their rumps upon its walls. Nobody noticed
what seemed obvious — there hadn't been necrotic buildings until recently. "Necrotic buildings have existed for
two hundred years," the local scholars claimed, but this
was bunk. Some magazines reported that Necrotic
Building Syndrome might have been responsible for
what were once considered war-torn structures. Maybe
there were never any wars but rather mass outbreaks of
NBS. "Don't tell us Belsen never happened," old-timers
complained. "Don't tell us we imagined the *Enola Gay*!"
The newscasts speculated about secret labs and home-
made pathogens and pigeon vectors. For years, our local
pigeons had been famously in love with the necrotic
building, making shit sculptures in the eaves that looked
like Munch paintings. The rec club was an eyesore but
the town had loved it just the same — or rather, claimed
it, even bitched about it, like a scapegoat child. The
mayor built it years ago for our community, but it had
withered long before the latest rot. It had facilities for
racquetball and squash and basketball. It housed a giant
swimming pool. It also had an ice rink where the children dreamed they'd be Olympians. One night our
favorite loudmouth, Buzz, had thought he'd be a hero
and gone in without protection to retrieve the children's
skates. Necrosis chewed off all his fingertips until his
hands were stumps. Or this was what the anchorpeople

said. "It's only mold," Buzz said into the camera. His eyes were swirly marbles and his matted beard looked like a succulent. "For Chrissakes, can't you see it's only mold?" The TV flickered off just as he'd laid that question in our heads. And then Buzz died. Or this is what the anchorpeople said. His time of death was never really known.

After that day, the town woke up, and there was a discernible transition in the air. The occupation of Zambonis perched around the borderlands, and the frigidity that had infected Jack began to spread to everyone. We grazed our mirrors, and they felt iced. We stroked our bellies and our thighs, and they felt nippy. We had given in to what the mayor said—his proclamation—and accepted that an oligarchic band of ice-resurfacing machines controlled the town. We talked of them like evil robots and then sometimes like paternal saints. We knew—the way a child knows—we should blame ourselves. We all had clumsy limbs and lived in houses made of cards. "My leg's asleep," I said to Jack, and he massaged it back to life. "Now it's my other leg. Perhaps I need resurfacing?" The worst part, though, was how we felt inside. Of course, I can speak only for myself. I felt completely dead inside. I felt like an inverted sunflower. Some numbness had invaded us, and most of us sat dormant in our homes all day until the clock struck six. And then we turned like sunflowers to watch the nightly news. "It's on!" I called to Jack. "The news."

The palliation was a huge relief. I wondered how we'd ever known the real from the unreal without the nightly news. We looked like heat-seeking explosives, honing on the glow of filled-up glass. At 6:05 they gave an update on the building and its rot. At 6:15 they talked to experts on Zamboni ice-resurfacing machines. The newscasts made us feel town pride. They made us ease into a sultry sleep.

Jack held my hand and stroked his cock as we

watched "Recreation Club: Our Fondest History," an hour-long special on TV. "Can you believe our town is famous now?" he asked. Some said our little town had been the epicenter of the outbreak of necrosis, and this bolstered tourism. We watched the Main Street bottle-necks on the TV. For years we'd tried to make ourselves as hip as bigger cities that had football teams. With earnest, laggard efforts we had tried to get the world to see that our Enormous Puppet Theater was something special, or our Klezmer and Gazpacho Festival. But no one cared. And then we found our niche: our town spawned a necrotic building. Yes! Our oeuvre was *destruction,* not gazpacho. Sure, we had been patsies, thinking our constructive efforts did a goddamn thing. Destruction did a world of good for our economy.

A panic settled in about the outbreak of necrosis, but we couldn't really focus on a single crisis out of two. We wondered if Necrotic Building Syndrome was communi-cable to another species—*us.* The nightly news reported any new inches of spread. They sent a man in a contam-ination suit to put some cameras inside, so we could watch the way necrosis overtook the staircase and the floors. After the showing of the creeping crud, an an-chorman would say a word or two about the way the "recent crisis had brought all of us together." Families ate their meals around a table now. Even the old-timers were glad for the revival of this once-extinct tradition.

When other townsfolk formed half-moons around their television sets, Jack pinned me to the bed and ripped my bra off with the TV humming in the back-ground. "My dick is throbbing hard," he said. He kissed my nipples hungrily and roughed me up. Abutting dis-solution turned him on. I struggled back at first. Then I broke down, grew flushed, and pooled with heat. "I've got to have your cock," I moaned. We fucked with zeal-otry because we fucked inside the struggle then. And this is why we watched the nightly news, despite the obvious contamination of our minds. It made us feel an urgency that we had lost. Our blood rose to our skin and we were flushed with life again. One night, we drove the car until we reached the rim of light, to see if the Zambonis were still there. We loved the way they witnessed us. Each time they didn't move, we felt we had defied them. They removed us from our intercellular war games for long enough to act as if we had an outer cell, an embassy.

As much as they policed us, we began to worship them. We told ourselves they were benevolent, they'd come for *us*. Without them we were riddled with our loathsome human weakness that we could not shed alone. We saw the glint of moonlight on their blades and thought about prismatic promises of light and liberty. We thought they represented hope, transcendence, transformation. We had once been young, our lives had once been good. We could go back to that if only they would scrape the awful epidermis of our selves to make a new reflective plane.

But then, they started moving in. The mayor—knowing that election day was coming up—had summoned them. "It's time," he said, at six. "We have to act before necrosis spreads to every building in our town." He asked the citizens to do their part. "Tomorrow afternoon, each one of you should grab a bucket or a hose," he said. "Each child can grab a sandpail. Flood the streets!" And suddenly, the able-bodied faction of the town was mobilized, and Jack and I were cowering in my room. "I'm scared," I said. We heard the sounds of hydrants breaking open, buckets spilling, chaos, then the calm of ice. They squabbled with each other as they poured the liquid down. The media were wrong. Of *course* there had been wars. There had been Belsen and Auschwitz and A-bombs dropped. It's just that wars had changed. There were no longer wars that were not civil wars, and we were—none of us—exempt. Jack tensely took my temperature again. "One hundred two point two," he said. He reached for the remote and turned the TV on again. The newscasts went on all the time.

That night at six with everything now sheathed in ice, an activist with dreadlocks grabbed the microphone and screamed, "It's mold! It's only mold!" but she was quickly swept away, the truth no longer relevant. We heard the ice-resurfacing machines advancing and we braced ourselves, both with anticipation and with fear. "It's time for a revival," said the mayor, cheerfully. "Let's welcome it!" They came in numbers—twenty, forty, more than anyone could count. They waited for us all to watch our etherizing dose of nightly news, to prep ourselves for city surgery, and then they rumbled into town. They scraped right down the icy streets, and we all watched them, mesmerized, until they nudged up to our lawns. Somehow we thought our borders—our own borders—were exempt. We saw Zambonis driving, unmanned, up our walks. We tried to run. We screamed when they pushed back our doors. We didn't think they'd come for *us*. But they had come. They pulverized our furniture, the picture of our Great Aunt Maude. They flushed us from where we hid beneath the furniture. We begged and pleaded: "Please just spare me! Don't choose me!" But they were robot soldiers, purposeful. We scrambled on the floors to get away, but still they barreled over us. They rolled us flat as sugar cookie dough. They squeezed our blood and lymph into a holding tank. They smoothed our curves and made us ruler-flat. They ironed us down upon our floors until we slept like AstroTurf slept on a winning field. Then the Zambonis rolled away and left us lying there.

We looked at our abraded, smoothed-out skin. We lay as flat as paper on our flattened floors, unsure of what to do. As daybreak hit, and we were sure we had survived, we suddenly felt lightened, free. We justified their actions and our pain. They had resurfaced us. We needed it. It was a gift! We'd shed our blood and lymph for freedom and community. We were a part of it—the fight for what was good. We watched the nightly news and thought how great it was that we could all be one, all paper dolls, each sublimated to this common cathode plane.

And then they rolled away.

My fever finally broke when it was ironed right out of me.

My eyelids flapped up like a classroom movie screen. My skin seemed like it had been ambushed by a cyclone, and my insides felt like they'd been poured with arsenic, then flushed. "Where are you, Jack?" I groaned. My blurry eyes made out the clock in front of me. I thought at first that it said "98.6" but it said "3:16 a.m." And then, from bed, I heard a *cracky-crack*. I recognized the sound of ice. My bones felt sore. My back felt processed like a sandwich that was made to look like ribs, but wasn't ribs and didn't taste like ribs. The TV hovered there in front of me, its gray screen asking for a light.

"Don't get the ice," I yelled to him. But then I realized the sound of ice cubes was no longer terrible to me. The noise was soothing, ringing like a set of wind chimes when the cubes hit glass. "Relax," Jack said, and strode into the room. "I'm just getting some juice." His alibi was sound—I saw the kitchen light through liquid in his hand. "Are you having Zamboni night terrors again?"

"I guess I am," I said. "Is that what's going on?" He climbed into the bed. His hand went down the smoothness of my cheek. "Shh, little Snoopy doll," he said. "I'll take your temperature again. Remember? It's been over 102 for two days now. You've been too sick to go outside." He stuck the little wand into my mouth and let it sit. And then he said, triumphantly, "It's 98.5!"

"Are the Zambonis gone?" I asked. He looked at me

a little cockeyed and he said, "Of course. The skating rink is done. They had the ribbon cutting." Then he touched my cheeks and said, "So icy cold and smooth." He smiled at me, as if his words were comforting.

"I mean," I said, now frustrated. "The occupation of Zambonis — has it left?"

"Calm down," Jack said. "You have no fever now."

He pulled me toward him for a kiss. Then he made love to me, but with his fleeting stamina. As soon as he began, he started rasping in and out, his exhalations grinding through his teeth. I could not think of anything but how he sounded like an ice-resurfacing machine. He rubbed on top of me, and seemed to say, "Zamboni." "What?" I asked. "Oh, honey," he repeated, rocking into me. He acted like he could squeeze out my insides with his machinist maneuvers on my flesh. Our bones weren't fitting right. They made an awful scraping noise, like dental tools on teeth. I audibly degraded from his touch. So then, I did what I had never done. I tried to tunnel free, but he was too oblivious to see. I took one fingernail and started chipping at the paint. Jack seemed a thousand miles away. "Oh, honey," he kept moaning blankly, but I only heard "Zamboni." Bits of paint and plaster rained on me from where I chipped. I couldn't stand how he moaned absently as cheap veneering fell. *Zamboni*, he exclaimed. *Zamboni, take me in*. I had a fantasy. I pictured Jack with needles and with ice cubes and a sterilizing fire. I thought how he could ice me down and pierce me on a dozen bits of skin, to make me feel again. That's when I started thinking about ice.

I didn't want to fuck. I only wanted ice-cube trays.

Around that time, a shudder rippled through his thighs. Jack came. "That was incredible," he said, as I spit out a paint chip that had landed on my tongue. I couldn't think of what to say. My words sunk deep beneath the place the chip had laid, as if the lead from it had run me through and ruined me.

ORIGAMI STRIPTEASE

Then, sated and switched off, Jack turned the TV on. The news reported on a bout of mold downtown and then, in closing, showed a video of a Zamboni moving snail-like on the skating rink. I saw the dissolution we had both become. I'd joined Jack's world. I was a block of ice for him to sculpt with heat and slipstream hands.

8.

The snow had come in hurling flakes, and then it melted off. The weather buoyed Jack's mood. We started doing things together. We started acting like a *couple.* I thought as long as I indulged his — granted — freaky peccadilloes, he would stick around. It was our eight-month anniversary, and he had some kind of surprise for me.

He took me to a warehouse area. He held his hands over my eyes and pushed me through a kitchen full of stainless steel that I could smell: it smelled like leaking spigots. "Don't open up your eyes," he said, then drew me to a stop. I heard the peeling suction sound and felt a rush of cold and sensed I must be standing near a walk-in freezer. "In you go," Jack said, and shoved me toward the cold. I stumbled forward on my toes. The metal door creaked shut behind me and the latch grabbed hold and I was breathing little clouds and trying to wring the cold out of my dishtowel hands. "You here, Jack?" I asked absently, but he did not respond. "Hello?"

I stood inside a hollow, lightless place. A deep sea, suffocating black. I opened up my eyes but there was nothing greeting them but cold. "Where are you, Jack?" I asked, now panicky. I patter-slapped the cans, the bags of flour and rice, the giant blocks of butter and the milk: the object Braille. Then suddenly, my body thudded on a block of ice. I tried to ascertain its shape. Its shape was human. It had muscles, curves, and sockets for its eyes. I thought he'd thrown me in a morgue at first, and screeched. And then the light flashed on. It was an odd, tenebrist light that beamed on frigid sculptures but left us in saturated dark. I saw the chunk of ice carved in a human form that emanated light with Caravaggio-like piety. Then there were animals — a panther, one coiled snake, a dozen swans — of ice. Jack grabbed me from the side and pulled me close against his warmth. "I wanted you to see my favorite place," said Jack. "I love it here."

"But why?" I asked.

"Enchantment. And because I've got the ax."

"The ax?"

"The ice pick. When each wedding's done they let me use the pick. The sculptor, my friend Franz, lets me do demolition on the ice. How do you like the ice menagerie?"

"It's mostly swans," I said. "Menagerie implies a bit more zoo."

I reached into the cold. The iceman's features were conspicuously melted off. His face looked like a picture of a baby's face in utero, the sockets and projections smoothed as if they weren't yet formed. He had a frozen codpiece where his icy balls and penis used to be. His concave belly was like crater-dented sand. His fingers had formed icicles that twisted toward the ground. This was the craziest of midnight sleep, but I was wide awake. "I wish we could be trapped in permafrost together," said Jack, wistfully. "It's like a time machine."

"I don't like how I feel here, Jack."

"Well, grab the man. Let's put him on the dolly."

The man and swan we took would not melt on their own, as it was twenty-eight degrees outside. We put them in the car but didn't turn the heat on. Jack strapped the swan upon the roof rack while I comforted the iceman. I talked to him like he was going to die. "Don't worry, iceman," I said to his caving eyes. "You probably made a lot of people happy at some gay or bachelorette soiree." The radio was on a crackling AM show on God. "Will you let Satan find a fissure in your faith?" the pundit growled. The cold sawed through the car. The longer we stayed on the road, and cold filled up my veins, and the AM radio was on, the more I felt a building rage at everything. How dare somebody mess with Jack's reality—my sweet and unassuming Jack. I was his gangster bride, the Bonnie to his Clyde. I'd flay the daily theater for him. I saw my role as ice avenger—taking on the numbing nihilistic world that turned Jack into this.

I wanted to decapitate the iceman, but it wouldn't be as easy as I thought. The lake was as unmoving as a stalker when our headlights wilted out. Jack started with the pick and hacked into a leg. The ice was hard as flagstone. Jack—already atrophied—could only knock a dime-sized divot out. "Let me try," I said giddily, though I was just as weak. The lake had framed the moon. The water wasn't frozen as the temperature had just dropped low that day. Because the cold had come so suddenly, my veins had snow-blind areas where no blood tried to go. I felt my body hiding from its corners as they suckled from the frost. Outside, the world's metabolism slowed into a frozen sleep. I hated it, the toothy ice that seized my assets like a sleazy Mormon's smile. I swung the pick against the iceman's face.

"Debaser," I yelled. "Blasphemer. You suck." I wanted to condemn him.

Then I struck his neck but nothing broke. The iceman clattered on the ground.

I started kicking him. I hacked and chopped and sumo-slapped the iceman but he did not give. I beat him with a stick and clawed at him and sat on him. I spat on him and called him names and tried to Psy Op him. But he would not degrade. "Jack, why is he so indestructible?" I asked. "Why won't he break?"

But Jack was sitting on a picnic table, rocking back and forth. His eyes were scratched with freezer burn. His lips were mumbling out a nonsense chant. The curved edge of the city shimmered like a gently rocking boat. Jack wouldn't even look at me. He curled up in a ball. "Just kill it, please," he moaned, and started trembling.

"I'll kill it for you, Jack," I said. "Don't worry honey. It will end."

I swung the pick and hit the iceman's heart and little diamonds of ice flew out but that was it. I couldn't kill the iceman, though I tried. I poked and kicked and rammed, but it would not break down. I felt an overwhelming sense of failure, and I knew that I was dueling over Jack. Not only was the iceman winning; he was colonizing limbs and claiming toes from me. Nobody would find evidence of how the iceman died, and history would triumph over us. "Take that," I yelled, and plunged a big stone on its head. The iceman rocked and bounced a little then lay flat.

"It is no use," said Jack. "We cannot win. So fuck it. Iceman cometh, iceman, gone."

"No, wait. I'll put it in the lake. How's that? It won't last there. It will dissolve like sherbet in a bowl of children's punch."

Jack grew more agitated. "*No,*" he said. "Someone will see it from a distance, and they'll think it is a child who drowned. I can't do that to anyone."

"It's just a sculpture made of ice," I argued. "Most people can tell."

"They can't," said Jack. "It is sadistic. There are missing children all the time."

"A child would not be big like this." I grabbed the iceman's leg and started dragging him. I wanted to be left alone with Jack, the swan, our trust. I wanted Jack to stop his craziness. "A child would not be so deformed or so translucent anyway." Jack grabbed my coat scruff and held on. His eyes were urgent when I spun around.

"*They will not know,*" he said. "They won't."

"Okay. Relax," I cooed. I squeezed his arm.

"The swan, though, has to go. The swan will dupe them pleasantly. Not like a frozen body in the lake. You'll see, it will look beautiful."

He pulled the car up to the edge of water and he took the bungee cords off the swan. We each stood by one wing and slid it down the hood and watched it splash into the water. There, it rocked a minute, toppled to the left and got its neck stuck in the frozen cattails on the side. I tried to turn it upright with a stick but Jack said, "No, we're running out of time. Let's go." The swan did not look beautiful at all. It looked like a mistake.

With that, Jack heaved the dirty, battered iceman back into the car. He started driving recklessly away. The gravel scattered underneath the bumper. "What are we going to do?" he shrilled, in agitation. "How will we find a place to dump it? God, it was an accident. You know that I'm not lying, right?"

"Of course I know," I answered, though I didn't know. I wished that he had taken me into a morgue, where things were definite.

"I didn't mean to do it, but it escalated. Things just slipped. I didn't—"

"Jack, I *know*." I touched his arm from where the iceman and I sat together, battling our internal thermostats.

"I'll take 142. The trees cut into radio around the quarry area."

The highway split into opposing lanes. Because there wasn't snow, but only cold that made illumination hibernate, the darkness formed two gloved hands on our necks. The highways there were lulling and, because oncoming cars did not turn off their brights until they got up in your face, you often saw some flashes of white dwarfs when animals could bound in out of nowhere and crush metal on their backs. Jack fiddled with the rearview mirror. At first we traveled silently, in tension. Then a ribbon of red light swept past the surface of the mirror and jumped back to Jack's face. "Oh shit, the cops," yelled Jack. His eyes went from the mirror to the wheel, and then he floored the gas. The iceman tilted forward then flopped back. The car raced down the road. The hood was joining prow to starboard of the darkness like a zipper pull. I turned my head to watch the red lights gaining, falling back, and gaining with their teasing bloody red.

ORIGAMI STRIPTEASE

"Why can't we give the iceman up?" I asked.

"We *can't,*" said Jack in frightened speech. "I think we're going to have to take it to the crematorium."

"Jack, listen, it's a block of ice. The crematorium is not the place for that."

"You want the cop to haul us in? You know of some-place else that has such contrary degrees?"

"Why would he haul us in? We haven't—"

"Because, in time there will be nothing here, no man, just water on our hands."

"So what?"

"We're made of water too. And limb to limb, a person cannot always differentiate."

We hugged the long bowed curve that passed the forest and the quarry on the left and then broke out into a great expanse of stretched-out fields. The car lights scanned the crowd of corn and then our ride choked out. The cop pulled right up at our side, and he was talking through his bullhorn at our car. His siren spit its red against the frost. "Pull over," said the cop. "Go hug the berm."

"Come on, Jack," I said soothingly. "The jig is up. I'll use my charms. Cops listen to cute girls. Can you just trust me?" I was smiling like an ice-cube tray.

As soon as I said "trust me," I could feel Jack soften up. "Okay, you're right. I'm freaking out," he said, and slowed the car, and steered it to the side. "I'm losing it." He laughed a nervous laugh.

The pig was fiddling with his badge. He shined his flashlight in our car. It went right through the iceman's head, which cast prismatic colors on the roof. The pig would see Jack's gender was ambiguous. The pig would probably beat him up. Jack hated cops, like all boys did. He didn't even know why he was running anymore. Where I saw obfuscation I could clear away, Jack saw the threat of hazing. He couldn't tell a meat locker from a crematorium. But I would handle this. I would make

Jack believe in me. I prettied up my skirt and licked my lips. "Good evening, officer," I said.

He waddled to the window and said, "Take your license out." He smelled like faded whiskey blotted out by food. As I began to bat my eyelashes, the cop slid up the beam and settled it upon the iceman's face. "My God," he screamed. His cornflake-pockmarked face sunk into milk. "You animals. You pervert sicko freaks. What have you done to him? That's Billy Marshall's kid." He slammed his fist against the hood. "That kid was going to be a hockey star." He paced five steps ahead, and grabbed his forehead, then paced back. I opened up my mouth to speak, but then the cop pulled back the door and yanked Jack out and punched him in the jaw and drew his gun, and I heard scuffling and a struggle and a bang. I saw Jack duck and heard the windows break and watched the glass collapse. The bullet must have grazed Jack's sleeve and hit the iceman's head, which shattered on my long, pink, faux-fur coat.

Jack stumbled for the car and turned the key and floored the gas. The cop was straightening his shot and looking for Jack's head, then dashing for his car. I opened up the other door and pushed the iceman out and watched the cop behind us, skidding on the shattered body's ice slick on the road. I looked down and saw blood from somewhere on my hands, but it was dark and I could not discern if it was Jack's blood or my own. The broken windows made the awful sound of woodwinds without reeds. Wind whistled through the unseen bloody gaps that suddenly had littered everything. I shivered. Red had vanished far behind us, down the drain of space.

"Out, out, damn cop," I said, and forced a laugh.

"What will we do the next time or the next?" asked Jack.

"We'll soak it into us," I said. "It's only water, Jack."

ORIGAMI STRIPTEASE

"It's not," said Jack. "It's more."

9.

As months between us piled into a structure I could lean against, they melted off. I started to feel jealous of the places that had surveyed borders. Plus, Jack never talked about another girl. He talked of Greenland. "That's where I've got to go," he said.

I thought that Jack would feel relieved when winter came and streets had turned to sheets of ice. I pictured cuddling with him under huge wool comforters. But February made him think of someplace more extreme. Jack spread out maps of Greenland, and he tacked them to the walls. He marked out exploration routes. He left for four days and told me he'd gone to see the northern lights. I knew that he was probably in a hospital performing stress tests or accessorized in magazines and Holter monitors. His health had gone downhill. His heart swelled like an overripe tomato, and his doctor said he'd need a transplant if it got much worse. Jack wanted to be somewhere that did not abide the sawtooth monitors that marked our time. He thought the cold would induce temporary hypothermia the way a surgeon did when he was trying to save somebody's heart from failure on an operating table.

He read brochures to me. "The northern lights are like a curtain flapping in the wind! There is no reason for a watch, so leave your time at home! Most months, the day has no beginning and no end. The sun hangs on a hook. The children ride their skates down streets all night, but midnight looks like day!"

"Why can't you take me with you there?" I asked. "It sounds so magical."

Greenland was an abstraction, a misleading birthmark on the map. It looked more like a spleen than heart. I knew he couldn't go to Greenland, nor could I—we were too sick, and we would perish there. But I was not

ORIGAMI STRIPTEASE

about to state the obvious—how frail we were, how far from everything. I knew that Greenland wasn't fur coats and suspended animation, and it wasn't an empirical snapshot of vivid breath. But it was his, and it was private, and I felt left out.

I whined. "I want to go to Greenland, Jack."

"Lie down, I'll snowshoe you right here," he soothed, and smiled.

I lay flat, and he climbed on top of me. I was the one who coined the term, *to snowshoe*, when I said that clumsy lovers always concentrate their flesh into a steely point. They flatten me beneath them with one rib or mole or elbow. Those who snowshoe spread out with an even distribution of their weight. Jack eased onto my flesh. "I want to go to Greenland," I said. "Please. Why won't you let me go with you?"

He read from a brochure to placate me. "The most spectacular attraction is the ice hotel!" he read. "The rooms are built of ice, surrounded by four sculptures that protect the crèche of sleep. The drinks aren't on the rocks—they're *in* the rocks, in glasses carved of ice!" He showed me pictures of the guests on beds of ice, in walls of ice, with glassy grins.

True, time had passed despite his efforts to freeze everything. Fall crept in with its fiddlehead of blown-up leaves, its shrunken face of bark. Then winter swirled in with its penchant for misdeeds. Each anarchist flake tumbled down, to build a government of sleep. I knew the nights would bleed under the snow with no trace left behind in morning. Then I slept and dreamed about the written Inuit in Greenland, still the only place the Inuit prefer to write their language down. I thought if we went there together, we could have historiography, a record of our trials. We could be mortared with our words, their ligaments or ligature—whichever it may be. I worried how my boy, so close to me, felt foreign all the time. I felt so exiled, pushed from skin by illness and its civil wars that turned related blood against related blood.

One night, Jack rocked my shoulders and he said, "Come on, I'm taking you."

He bundled me in long johns, flannel shirts, lined jeans, and wool, then steered me to the door. I stumbled sleepily. One stubborn horse blew cold out of its nose. Hitched to a sleigh, the horse took us into the woods and there, beside a cabin, was a dogsled. The dogsled pulled us in our reindeer pelts across the field of white.

The night was spinning on its turntable. Jack mushed the dogs and held my hand beneath the pelt. The trees were groping for lost glasses underneath the snow because there was no light and a pervasive feeling that there wouldn't be another light. I started to feel nervous. Had I pressured Jack? The country wasn't his, was not a colony of ours, and wasn't green. But he'd called dibs on it, and I had never thought of Greenland, not until I felt like Jack had married into symbols that weren't mine. I didn't care about the plight of arctic wolves and, when I thought of what I wanted, it was fire, not ice. So why did I think I had any claim to Greenland now? I felt a sense of dread. Perhaps we would get lost in Greenland and would not return. It was the kind of night when snow eats breadcrumbs and it has no hunger for the piquant rainbows of the dawn. How were we navigating? Dogs? External dogs? I looked around, and nothing felt familiar in this field. Jack led the dogs with tiny gestures that seemed almost like telepathy.

In truth, I was completely threatened, eaten up with jealousy each time I saw a map. I thought that Greenland, like all countries, was a woman. Jack must have felt a love for glaciers that he didn't feel for me. No *real* girl could compete with the mystique of icebergs, even with taunting hoop of skirt. This country altered time, and I could not do that. I couldn't comfort him. I couldn't lie to Jack and tell him it was light when it was dark. I couldn't change the X-ray truth that shone through us, our bodies, like a bomb that burned an effervescent life into a shadow on the wall. I couldn't give him exports, whores, and molybdenum fields. I wasn't half as good as Greenland, and this made me insecure.

Amazingly, I wasn't cold. The silence and the darkness smudged away my sense of time.

The slick terrain was stretching aimlessly, and I began to nod off into sleep. Jack handed me a thermos and he told me, "Drink." The tea tasted like an old suede coat brewed up with maple bark. The taste was awful, but it heated up my stomach. I felt my eyes turn into jack-o'-lanterns, then they drooped off into sleep. I slept a lost, uncharted sleep. I opened up my eyes, and I was in the center of an igloo. I glanced outside, surprised. The dogs were lying in a circle like a string of lights around the cold perimeter.

"After you stack the blocks you heat the belly up inside and open up the door and let the cold air in so that there is a sheath of insulating ice," he said. "That's what protects you from the cold." I gawked at him, surprised that he had pulled it off.

"Are we in Greenland?" I asked Jack.

"Of course," said Jack, delighted that I knew. "Glance out and tell me if you see the northern lights. I bet they're there."

I wanted to have faith that somehow, we'd arrived. I stared outside again, and squinted up my eyes, and tried to see. When both my lids were squeezed to slits, and I distorted starlight through my snow-touched eyelashes, I saw a little bit of blue, then red. I told myself I saw the northern lights.

"I see them!" I exclaimed.

"They're beautiful. They are so marvelous," he said. He started crying, and I held him.

"Yes, they are," I answered him.

He grabbed my hands. "So now you understand.

PEGGY MUNSON

You see." He gazed at me sincerely, hungrily.

I nodded earnestly. I wanted to believe we were in Greenland. Sadly, it was obvious we weren't. There hadn't been a plane or boat, and Greenland was an island. Still, I wrapped the reindeer pelts around his shrinking body, and I held one warm hand on his heart. He sobbed out quiet tears, and I was scared the drama of it was too much for someone with a broken set of pumps and valves inside. I wasn't going to tell a dying child there was no Santa Claus.

"Shh, Jack, relax. You are enveloped in the northern lights. You saw them, right?"

"Well, yeah," said Jack. He wiped his nose. "They are my favorite part."

"Nobody knows you're here. You're safe."

I hugged his body tight against my body as he wept. I knew what Greenland was. It was Jack's way of saying, "If I go, you'll never locate me again." I thought if I just played along forever, he would stay. I'd learn the shape of his illusion. In time, I'd sleep inside the ice hotel. I'd know.

"You're beautiful in Greenland," Jack said, kissing both my eyelids.

What did I know? I'd never been outside the fifty states. The Lapland lemmings sounded like a myth to me as well. But why? Because they followed blindly, with a faith I couldn't comprehend? Some people married in a distant chapel made of ice. The chapel was inside the complex of the famous ice hotel, and I had *seen* the photographs of it in Jack's brochures. It was as luminous as you'd imagine, heavenly. Should I discount those wedding vows because the chapel melted once a year and had to be rebuilt? Was I that cynical?

"You should lie back. I'll snowshoe you," I said.

I laced my fingers into his and climbed on top of him. I reached beneath my pelvic bone and opened up his jeans. I pulled his cock out of the pee hole in his boxers. Then I rode on it. I hoped that sex would bring us close again. I was compressing our reality within the blinders of a motion. It was not different from a child's desire to put a snowball in the freezer to prolong the magic of a season. I felt his jeans against my clit, the sanding of my nerves. I didn't notice that the walls were melting, if they were.

"Come on, Jack, come into my little space," I said.

I reached under his ass to pull his cock up into me. He started entering his entering. "Your body is an ice hotel to me," said Jack.

I'd never been to Greenland, but I knew that it was there.

I curled up next to him and slept. I dreamed the igloo drifted off atop an ice floe, but I was alone, trapped in the sudden absence of Jack's warmth. I crawled out from the little igloo hatch and saw him on another floe. The night-black water pushed our bodies far apart. Jack waved at me. I tried to lift my hand but, suddenly, my arms had turned to icicles. I tried to speak but then my mouth was ice — flash-frozen like the belly of the igloo.

"You are a snapshot there," Jack shouted from his drifting floe. "I hope you stay like that, unmoving in my mind."

I watched his eager body wave as it got smaller in the distance, broken off from me. The snow obscured his face. Jack was a snowflake; that was all.

"Goodbye," he yelled. "My ice hotel. My frozen refuge. Ciao."

I saw the ice. The positive against the negative.

I saw the positive.

10.

The last time we fucked, he took me to a cemetery. There were two tombstones of children, raised and flat as holy books on pedestals, covered by a couple dozen weathered toys. "Lie down on it," said Jack, and pointed to the girl's stone. I did as I was told. I climbed up on the stone. It was too small for me. Both stones were about the size of cribs. I had to put my knees up. The sky escaped above me like a pool of excess hair dye swirling down a drain. Crows were scattering like blowing ash, as if they were foreshadowing, the way crows do. Jack grabbed my chin and said, "Now close your eyes and think as if you're fighting not to die." Jack and I did not have to make metaphors of broken hearts. We both had cardiologists waiting for us to prove them right.

I wanted to cry because the girl was dead and all her toys were starting to look like shrunken heads. Jack took his fingertips and touched me where my belly met my waistline. He slid my shirt up so I felt the breeze. His lips were moving half an inch above my skin. "Spirits," said Jack to my belly. "Spirits," said his lips. The sound of dry leaves scratching against the cemetery road felt like a rake against my spine. Jack pinched my nipples hard and pressed his lips against my lips, and then he grabbed me by the neck and choked me, violently, for just a second. I gasped and then he reached down, and his fingers diddled on my pussy, and he said, "You are the sickest bitch. Your pussy's wet from this." I felt ashamed, just like he wanted me to feel.

I felt ashamed each time he looked at me. Each work of theater is pivoting upon embarrassment. That's what my playwright friend said. This tension is what keeps us in our seats. As if we're all afraid we'll be revealed, or there will be a person stuttering, or lights will flood the places we've been hiding in our minds. We're all afraid that theater is real, and real is theater, and all of it is shamefully revealing. Yes, Jack looked at me too long, the way conquistadores move figurines around a military map, as if I were a game of chess. He looked at me until my words were jagged, torn up into bits, and catching like a fishhook every time I tried to spit them out. I couldn't even talk to him. He made me fall apart with just a look. The way that buoy sounds like boy, and there is nothing else to grab.

And Jack looked beautiful. It was a word he'd hate, but he looked beautiful, with lips that could have ended wars and shallow lines around his eyes, the way retreating water cracks the sand like clawing fingers. I knew he wasn't mine, but I could not relinquish him. The light was tickling us, its mirrored movement in and out of trees, and we drove to the area where tombstones sloped off toward the river. The factories across the river looked so brilliant from the way that they reflected light. "Pull," the coxswain screamed behind us from a sculling shell, the rowers cranking back in unison, "*pull.*"

Jack told me once, when he was weakening, that I had lips that looked like they were born to suck cock. He sat there on the hood of the car, one boot on the bumper, and his cock was there, subterranean pressure, under his Levi's. "Pull," he said to me in just a whisper, put my fingers on his zipper. I wanted to use my teeth. I put my hand around his cock. I squeezed his balls. I pulled the zipper open and his denim gasped but we stayed quiet. We were afraid to feel.

It's as if I made this up. The coxswain yelling "pull" as my mouth slid down on his cock. *Coxswain*, from the French for *cockboat* and for *servant*. Small boat, and boy servant, *swain*. Cocksucker for the motion of marine spray. Small swallower of deadly swells. I sucked Jack's cock like I could keep him there, but he was staring across the water. My knees were pressing into tiny rocks. My shirt was riding up above the license plate. My skirt was rustling against my pussy, which was dying to lure his cock down from my mouth. I held him by the thighs and sucked. He grabbed my hair and whispered, "Yes, baby, that's it, that's it." He watched the human water-bugs glide over the water. Behind us were a thousand deaths. And it was near the end for us: the crows were scattering everywhere and then regrouping. The crows were getting ready to end the day.

And then there was a path, a frantic path that cut along the water but was hidden by the shallow water plants. And Jack was ripping up my skirt along the roots. And he was choking me with crowded nourishment, and he was pushing back my shameful wisp of panties and was cursing, "Fucking slutty whore, I need to fuck you *now*, so stop resisting me." He slapped me with his hand, and then he ripped his belt out of its loops the way a father does when he is going to lash his child and then he looped the belt into a noose and put it over my throat and pulled me backward along the trail with it until I tried to fight him and I pushed and kicked and shoved and tried to breathe. And then he loosened it and plowed his cock into me and all the animosity of nature bloomed into a star. And then he fucked me tenderly as if the rest of it was just a joke. He fucked me like he loved my pussy more than any room he'd ever tried to work.

I'm lying still as if I'm in a coma. A coma, if it doesn't kill you, heals whatever's wrong. It's dark, the aftermath of Jack. Each day I wake as if I sucked his cock and then the car rolled over me. Each day I lift myself from under cars. I'm left for dead but never die. And this I do mean literally. Jack's illness and my illness made us tilt when we were walking, angling off like peg-legged pirates. Perhaps our skewed direction made us orient to moons instead of suns, to people who were not so much like us. We were like monarch butterflies, dying several times in each migration. We were like many incarnations pressed into a single life. We fucked people as if we had to steal their bodies.

And then Jack's letter came. It drifted down as white as sugar on a day of insulin restraint. It said a little bit but not a lot. "I've written you a thousand letters, but they all distilled into this one," it said. "And you distilled into the mad elixir that's killing me when I'm away." But then the words infected me, so beautiful and parasitic, and I couldn't think of anyone but Jack. I tried. I had a boy squeeze water from a sponge over my hair and face, and all the while he did I wished that Jack could come and leave me pregnant, so I'd have a piece of him to keep. Of course, immaculate conception didn't come from rogues. Jack's cock, as well as it was engineered by NASA and as well as he could cleave through outer space, could not make little Jacks. The boy used boar's hair brushes on my back and feet and tender places. "Ma'am?" he said, and offered me a towel. He rubbed me up and down and led me to the bedroom where the pillows had been fluffed. The boy knew nothing but to be too kind.

But just as he began to rub me down with almond oil, the doorbell rang. The boy said, "Ma'am? Are you expecting company?"

"Get rid of them," I said, and shooed him toward the door. I heard the sound of mumbling.

"They won't be rid," the boy said when he came back to the doorway. Jack stood there with a smirk and blindfold. "I'm sorry, Ma'am," the boy said when he wrestled me and helped Jack put the blindfold on. He clicked the handcuffs on my wrists. "I truly am." But I was not surprised. Jack got to everyone. Jack showed up only when his terms were biblically carved. He turned all people into scraps. The boy—like every boy—preferred to be a cartoon in a gum wrapper, ensconcing his small caricatures and lore and pinking cheeks in waxy refuse, wafting off whenever it got breezy. The boy just loved to bow and backward-walk away.

Then darkness started, all degrees of it. Jack shoved me into his pickup, hooked my handcuffs to a dog chain in the back. I rattled all the way to somewhere, and I pressed my cheek against the glass although I knew I couldn't smell or hear him. I was a needy and neglected dog. I became nauseous from the rattling, and I needed medication, and I couldn't walk at all when he stopped near the smell of fresh-cut grass. Jack held me up, and I was stumbling forward, and my hands were desperate for a stone of any kind. He later told me that he fucked me over Freelove's headstone but I'll never know for sure because he didn't take my blindfold off. First, he led me to the faggy angel—this I recognized. He made me feel the angel's quadriceps and lick its lap. He made me touch the lacy ornate cutouts at the top of skinny markers. Then he held me back against his chest, and I could smell him, feel his cock against me, and his lips pressed downy hairs against my neck. That's what I wanted, just to sink against his chest, but there we were—amidst dark truth, the transience of everything.

Of course it wasn't easy. It was rough. We struggled. Jack put the handcuffs on me again and then let go of me. "Go," he said, and shoved me, "This will be a foxhunt." I stumbled forward, and he laughed behind me. I could hear his footfalls and his rest, and I was almost tripping, banging into headstones, through the dark, as if he was a killer and I had to run from him. And this was crazy, we both knew it—invalids pursuing invalids. I felt him hurrying up behind me, then he grabbed me and he threw me over the stone and yanked my pants down to my knees and took his knife and ripped my panties off. The ripping sound, its sacrilege, caused birds to burst into a racket as they scattered from the trees. They all refused to witness this. "Spirits," said Jack as he slid his cock into my ass. "I hope the spirits will forgive us."

It's as if I made this up; it was so many worlds ago.

ORIGAMI STRIPTEASE

He rode me quietly, in tense restraint. Our bodies warmed against the friction of the stone, like we were knives. I told myself when Jack was moving his exquisite cock: *I won't come back here, like I'm saying Kaddish, every year. I will not let his usual chicanery unravel me.* Jack whispered in my hair, "A woman makes a graceful entrance, and a guy—a guy wins when he makes a perfect exit." He fucked me like he loved me and would never go. "Push," I said to him. "Just push inside of me." And so he did—he pushed inside my bawdy old saloon, and everything revolved around a metal heat, and all the doors were nondirectional. His cock was right where it belonged and we both knew it, but I also knew that he would leave. He might return, and maybe one day, stay. But neither one of us could quite forgo the idolatry of kites.

And this is how I came to wait, and close myself into this pining box. I licked the backs of postage stamps as if they were his cock. I only needed homeopathy, a few words here and there, his scattered penned-in sentences. A letter could be like a perfect surgery. I told myself I knew what he was thinking when he walked through stony wordless days. I told myself we were the same— two people who packed dynamite into our small admissions. Of course I could find lovers who would grant me gushy words of praise. And so could Jack: I'm sure he did. We looked at them like they were bags of blood, and weren't they, really, that? A part of us was drawn to rosy cheeks, to chattering devotion. But Jack and I would die for just one perfect word, one perfect place to rest. And so I waited for another night when we could be alive, reborn, enlaced. I knew he'd be back home. Because my body—we both knew it—was Jack's final resting place.

Part 2:
If She Is Falling into Animal

1.

The door had lost its marrow, so it made a sound like breaking skeet. Because I hadn't had a visitor for so long I thought, for just a moment, I heard my neighbors shooting blanks.

Krack krack krack. "Anybody home?"

The Sludge was leaning on his black guitar case, five fingers twined around a small bouquet. His face was boyishly self-deprecating, and he hung his head when I eased back the door. "Before you slam my violets in the door, I came to say I'm sorry," said The Sludge. "Not just with empty words but reparations. I want to fix what I have done." I'd thought about a hundred speeches I would give to him, a hundred martial arts moves I would use, but suddenly I was a mute girl with hysterical paralysis. He didn't seem as monstrous as I remembered him. His hands were not so lobster-like; more like a seaman's hands worn down by rope. He pulled a plastic case out of his bag. "I write with pencil now," he said, as if that proved he'd changed.

I nearly fainted in the doorframe. "Aren't you a sight to make my sore eyes blind," I sputtered out.

"I'll ail what cures you, and I'll cure what ails you," said The Sludge.

I heard The Sludge had gone away to terrorize another town of girls. Of course, I had a curiosity to see what would become of him—I think it's natural to ponder someone's villainy if you have been a victim. When I was generous, I wondered if he had a gentler side, if he was more dimensional, since all I knew of him was sketchy and so painful. The only thing more intimate than violence is death, and The Sludge had been the only witness to my dissolution. He shared a closeness with my illness that few people shared. I wondered if he did desire redemption. I kept the door opened a crack and only that.

"But are the pencils lead?" I asked.

"I can assure you, no," he said, and smiled. He didn't step my way but leaned his body forward. "Graphite."

"You're close enough," I snapped. I pulled my robe a little tighter. Cold crept around The Sludge's body, through my door and up my legs. I then remembered how he carried weather with him like a hoodwinked kite. My anger hardened my resolve to keep him out. But suddenly, The Sludge began to cry. His heap of flesh hunched over like a molten Thinker carved of wax. He sobbed in labored swells. Then with a sharp intake of breath, the torrent stopped abruptly. He started talking in a rapid fire of syllables. "You see," he said, "when we first met, I was the sewage of a lifetime of unwritten words. I grew up living hard. My world was full of users who would always be unformed. They fell into the drink when they were young and were so soppy all the colors of my family portrait ran. I wandered through a labyrinth of shallow drowning spots, a shot-glass sump. I knew one thing: I'd choke on my own unexpressed emotions if I didn't find a way to get them out. I thought you could articulate the things I couldn't say. I should have loved you, but instead I felt a jealousy that sawed me into thirds. That's why I went to look for you. What I wanted was to swallow you, the way that you could write things down, not make you swallow me. I wanted what you had inside. Instead, I gave you mine, what I was made of, poison through and through. I made you suck the venom out of me." His sobbing grew intense. I thought to leave the door to get a tissue, but I quickly thought the better of it. It troubled me that I felt sympathy at all.

"I didn't mean to poison you," he said. "I meant to show you *me*. I thought you could take all the ink I had inside and turn it into something beautiful. The way I gave it was a travesty. My inclination was to open up myself and hope that you could be the one to love me and transform me. I know now it was harmful and absurd. But maybe some of us are made of cyanide and not of blood. Maybe some of us have rhythm but no words."

I felt a sudden surge of anger at him then. I opened up the door. With all my might, I shoved The Sludge away from me. His balance wasn't good, but he was also not so stiff that he might topple over. He wobbled then regained his poise. I clutched my chest and started coughing. "See now?" I was yelling. "Even that—my hate—exhausts me now."

"I am so sorry," said The Sludge. "I am." His eyes were luminous as the eyes of fish. He looked as innocent and dumb as brine shrimp in a tank. "But please, just hear me out. I have your answer. It is not a vial of potion but more genuine. You see, sometimes the poison is the antidote. You need someone to dote on you, someone who owes you now. I think that I can undo what I did. If you will only let me in—"

I looked at him a long, long time, the way the moon stares down the sun and neither really wins the trump but somehow, they acknowledge they are inexorably related. Then he played his ace: "Who else has motive to repair you now? Who else will help?" I knew The Sludge and I were meant to know each other then, and in that moment, I eased back the door. He marched right through as if he'd practiced that cue a hundred times.

Almost instantly, I felt regret, but he—once in my house—became a snake-oil salesman, spinning me around his words so I was rapt. "We're going to fix you up," he said. "Do you need food? Do you like pasta dishes? Is this light fixture broken?" He shuffled by me, and he started trying to assess my needs. "I really want to do so many helpful things," he said.

By then, as sick as I'd become, my life of fantasy was

all I had to keep me going. I could have walked into a Kool-Aid cult right then, and he at least had strong arms and a willing back. I knew that he *could* help me if he *really* wanted to—and who else would? I put my faith in him the way that desperate people listen to a charlatan and pay to bathe in sulfur springs, not noticing—or just ignoring—how their bodies smell like rotten eggs. The Sludge was like a smell that would not leave my skin no matter how I scrubbed, but still, I thought, perhaps the properties of my revulsion had the paradoxical ability to heal.

Besides, The Sludge was handsome. He was a flickering neon light above a basement bar that hummed with human life and lust.

I thought it wouldn't hurt to see what kind of suction he was selling—even if it left my floors a mess or filled the air with fine amnestic dust.

I felt a strange descending calm as soon as he arrived. He snored beneath a single ratty blanket I had given him. At first, I simply stared, but then I crept into his room and curled beside his body. He slid around and held me while I slept. He shooed my dictators of sleep away. The night was as rewarding as a lucid dream in which I finally speared a dragon. By morning, he had ground fresh coffee beans and made pancake batter. "Look," he said, and pointed to the table. "Look, I got you that." There was a journal there. It was exactly like a leather-bound one Jack had given me. I opened it and all the pages were still white. I thought at first—absurdly—that The Sludge had simply wiped my old one clean, had rubbed it white with both his awkward thumbs. But this was lunacy. "Here's to our new beginning," said The Sludge, and raised his orange juice glass.

There is a reason for the saying about keeping enemies in close proximity. To know a monster's whereabouts is much less frightening than not knowing where he is. With mine so near, I wasn't dodging every shadow in my way. Sometimes the only thing a person has is the belief that demons want to be redeemed. When he had poisoned me, The Sludge had filled me with a sick teratogenesis that couldn't be expunged—the monster-baby of his ink. I wanted him, the forceps of his violence, to get it out. I knew one truth: though Gods may make us, monsters often form us. I thought if he could break me all the way, if he could rip me into my component parts, then I might heal. I thought if he could be redeemed—someone so vile—then so could I.

And this is why, when he leaned in his head, I let him plant his lips on mine, and let mine feel the pressure and the giving in.

We kissed and pulled away and then, engulfed in peacetime, broke into our separate smiles. He leaned in with his thumb and wiped a smudge of lipstick from my chin.

I only meant to hear him out, to give him momentary charity, but charity—like anything—can spin out of control. I know that what I did seems stupid, like I courted my own hell. But think about ingredients of gain and loss. Sometimes a synergy is made from dubious bedfellows. I couldn't run away from terror when it chased me down. I had to fold my illness into me. Once I had kneaded all I had into a Frankenstein-formed pie, I had to eat the whole. I had no choice; it was my own. Some people have the luxury of scooping out the sun inside a moon-shaped eggshell, segregating it. Some people herd their Dobermans behind a chain-link fence. I didn't have this luxury. The landscape changes utterly when one is sick, so that the most unreasonable cures seem sensible. Thus, animals chew batteries and tires and plastic bags if they eat poisoned meat, to try and get the poison out. When one has something inside that needs rubbing off, it seems a good idea to eat sandpaper. And furthermore, the notion of a real apology was just as temping as religion then. The Sludge was oozing with charisma, like a minister from a revival tent. My illness beat me down. It changed the lipids of my brain. It acted on me like cult programming from deep within my cells. The way my sleep was chopped up into bits, and I went weeks sometimes too sickly to get up to take my vitamins. I was malnourished, also, from the daily gruel of my own deprivation. Eventually, an illness turns the sanest person into a hysteric, even when she isn't one. It makes a person think that she is Joan of Arc, a wasting girl who falls asleep to visions. When Joan chose grandiosity to girlhood, the choice made perfect sense. In that equation, in that period of time, wasn't her grandiosity the logical antithesis of girl? It's when we realize that we are limited that we become as hysterical as God. We turn into a Kodachrome, magniloquent production, rife with hellfire, floods, and miracles, upon an isolated stage. And if a single definition were our only option—if a girl could only be a dress blown up by any wind—then we would all go mad. Sometimes, if monsters are a necessary consequence, we have to choke them down and then redress.

That's why I let my enemy into my house. To understand why forces that created both of us turned both of us to miscreations.

"Well, I'm glad you're here," I said to him.

He nodded, feigning empathy, his smile a toppled moon, a sickle coming down.

2.

And so the days passed on assembly lines, efficiently contained in well-marked packaging. Initially, The Sludge seemed like a godsend. He was as good to me as he had once been bad. I heard him whistling bluegrass tunes and banging pots. "I made your favorite cast-iron cornbread and some soup," he said, as I dragged out my leaden body from the other room. He'd ironed his shirt so that it stood up like a crimped zoomorphic napkin. The Sludge dressed up each day for me, though I looked ragged, wan, and disparate. I slid in like a draft.

"The kind that's crusty on the side? Then drenched in maple syrup?" Among his attributes, The Sludge cooked home-style food like no one else.

"The syrup's from Vermont and tapped so fresh it's practically a psychedelic," said The Sludge. "I bought it from the farm store down the road." He knew I used my cornbread as a sponge. He had a memory for my particulars and quirks.

The Sludge and I were more simpatico than I imagined we could be. Some days, forgiveness filled my heart with lightness when I looked at him. My own forgiveness was a window into metamorphosis, one symptomatic cure, and part of me thought that it paved the way to fuller, more holistic cures. But this idea was misled. The newly buoyant parts of me were pushed by tidal forces of The Sludge's brooding anger and my own. A part of me—the part that smelled the putrid stench of rotten eggs, knew surely, I was nearing jagged rocks. I thought because The Sludge had damaged me that he could *know* me, know me better than another could. That he could find the reason, fix the root. Each one of us has lived a different hell, and how can one translate a fire to someone locked in ice? One can't, and that's why fiery hells seek fiery hells.

99

PEGGY MUNSON

The Sludge seemed changed. I don't think it was just a show. The act of my forgiveness made him feel redeemed. He had a new bounce in his step. He brought me Belgian chocolates, and he fed me from the box. He wore an apron when he swept the floor and chopped the basil and the pine nuts for his pesto. We only once made love, and that was part of why I trusted he was looking out for me. He told me, "Don't exert yourself like that. You have to heal." But there was that one time, the night that my forgiveness had crescendoed into something like desire. The Sludge was trying to sleep, but I awakened him. I already felt jealous of the secrets in his dreams. He rolled over and kissed me, and he touched my hair.

"You have to fuck me," I said to The Sludge. "I want you to make love to me."

His eyes were spinning out with hunger, then turned kind. "We shouldn't do that, should we? I can't ruin you again."

The Sludge slept—sometimes—with his cock attached, and this night I reached down between his legs but there was nothing there. He got embarrassed. "Wait," he said. "Hold on. I have to get it."

When I felt the absence there, he suddenly seemed needier than ever. His absence triggered mine, so my whole body was unbarred. Minutes later, he was back in bed and prodding me with something sizable and stiff. I knew I wasn't going to suck on it, but he was grabbing at my butt and pulling me. I had to feel his dick inside of me. It was the distillation of his force and thus, I had to know it. That force and what it held was part of my great mystery—it was the vehemence that underpinned the birth of my worst hell. "I've waited for so long for this," he said. "I have been dying with want." He slid the cock inside of me. Between us was a strange abstraction, something hovering between our flesh that unified our separate beliefs. It was the way that we contained it, pressed it in a form—this sweet abstraction, this imagi-

nary thing—that made me feel I almost grasped the esoteric in that moment. We were not merely making love.
We were compacting our ideas into ideology. If I could
grasp and meld the esoteric, I could heal from it. I
thought.

The Sludge knew that I liked it rough, but this time,
he was gentle. He cooed into my ear, "You're marvelous.
You're like a stolen painting." He slid his cock inside me
slowly, and I felt like I was climbing up a winding staircase to a nebulous escape. He turned me over then and
pried his way into my ass. "Come on, come on," he said.
"That's it." The sex was good, too good. It seemed to fill
The Sludge with fear. The next day, when I saw him, he
looked panicked. "Have some toast," he said. He seemed
more hunched and waddling. He touched my cheek and
shook his head. We never talked of how he whispered
blank checks of confessions in my ear. He'd said, "I felt
such adoration for you from just reading you. I read each
word you wrote, from here to Detroit and beyond."

But afterward, it was the wordless space that capti-
vated me. He'd gone into the place that lived behind our
limited constructions of the skin and all that it supposed-
ly delineated.

There was another reason why I opened up my house to
him. I don't know why Jack ran from me, but I felt empty
and erased. I did know this: some people can see demons
on the screens of children's eyelids. A part of me had
wondered what horrific thing Jack saw in me. If there
was some essential evil there, a thing that made Jack run,
I knew The Sludge would fish it out. I had no question in
my mind that what he found in me—no matter how
demonic, how traumatic or revolting—it wouldn't make
him flee. He would embrace it, take it in, the way that I
absorbed his ink. The Sludge would sop it up the way an
oily hole in space sops up a galaxy. There is no metamorphosis without inversion, shedding, turning out. I

needed him.

I needed him because I wasn't whole. I sat in a cocoon of my own body, waiting to be hatched. If nature or The Sludge had wanted me to die, I would have died when I initially got sick. Instead the pause in animation seemed to indicate that I'd been tapped for transformation, that—if I could heal—I would emerge a blue and purple palette poised for flight. In this depiction, he was not a villain, really, but the catalyst. Perhaps The Sludge could coax me into flight. I needed to believe I was a metamorph.

With this, forgiveness and redemption served the two of us. Some nights he came into my room and wanted sex, but I turned him away. Some nights I curled up next to him and slept. We got to know the gentle curves of eyelashes, the signals they transmitted. One final night he came to my room, I simply waved him off. He didn't come to me again, and then a strange thing happened. Then, I wanted him. I yearned for him. I yearned for what I felt between his legs that night, his boyish shame of what he didn't have. He made me omelets and he ladled out my soup, and nothing filled my hunger for the absence. Oblivion was there: it called me with its mournful loons.

I started begging at his door. I stood there wide-eyed, empty as a cauldron. I didn't know—not then—how much he liked it when I begged. He didn't shame me for my incompleteness. While New Age preachers emphasized the primacy of self, he welcomed my dependency, and my dependency was not a psychological pathology. It was as real as the dependency of wheelchairs on their ramps. He knew about not being whole. What wasn't there between his legs that night, what someone more creative than The Sludge could just create, he yearned for as a stump yearns for a phantom tree.

It's true we only made love once, but by "made love" I mean The Sludge had touched me gently and with love.

Other times, we fucked haphazardly. He held me to the wall. He said, "You're going to take it," and I did. He did it rough, the way I liked. We didn't kiss. We needed violence to create a distance. Sure, we could have loved our enemies, but it felt better to mine pleasure from the wreckage in their eyes. Some nights, he slapped me, and he pinched my nipples hard. I liked it when he roughed me up. It turned me on. I let him know it did. I told him that he made the saplings bow and bluebells curtsy, like a demigod of wind.

Those nights, he foraged in the old ingested inkblot he had made. It was a riddle that we tried to know by touch, but couldn't know. We tried to pull the inner terror out of me, to purge. Some nights, when he pushed up in me, my insides were an oil slick oozing over a conspiracy of ravens.

"I know," he said, as if to soothe a crying child. "I know."

When I began to fear he might be evil, he was kind. He watched me while I slept, the way that one might mind a field of corn, though nothing happened but the rustle of some genes. He worried over me. When I could not stand up, too goddamned weak, he braced my body to the other room. When I was cold, he pulled the covers over me. Then moments later, when I felt a wash of heat, he drew them off. He never made me feel ashamed that I was sick. The Sludge was better than a lot of people, most, at dealing with my illness. He came with buckets when I had to puke. He held my hair back, and he wiped my mouth when I was done. Nobody else had cared for me like that.

He also nursed my grief. Some times I thrashed around. "I hate it here," I cried. "I hate how sick I am. I cannot fucking take it anymore."

"I know," he said, and stroked my head. "I know." At times, I looked at him and wondered how he'd ever been the beast I knew before. But then, some nights, I felt the animal in him, the way he loved to pin me down and make me want. I felt some comfort knowing I could see his different parts. That way, there were no rooms of predators I didn't apprehend.

To understand the impact of one soul's compassion, it is important to know this: I got a lot of flack for being sick. When someone doesn't die, but lingers on, it starts to look suspicious. Most people blamed the victim even when a causal agent could be found. They were believers in the triumph of a person's will. They felt I didn't have a certain type of fortitude. They had a stealth theology that judged the ill. They thought I was wisteria and estrogen. They *knew* my attitude was bad. I let The Sludge into my life because I hoped to rein the illness in a separate room. My illness *was* a sludge-like thing. He was its moniker and patriarch. It's true that I lacked will in certain ways. I could not keep a fast or give up sugar, for example. Plus, I'd surely done some morally distasteful things. By then, though, every doctor knew that I was sick. They had the blood tests and the charts. They didn't doubt how bad it was but scratched their heads, unsure of how to help. What's more, the worse I felt, I couldn't even travel in a car to them. Their offices were far away, and none of their injections seemed to help. The Sludge had done more for me than the mute of hounds that were the doctors and their scratching posts. He gave me what I needed and—because I had my pride—he made me feel like I was giving something back. He also knew that being bedridden so much had made me think of many ways to fuck. He never stopped reminding me how much he owed me for the damage he had done.

"I've got your favorite drug," he teased, and framed me on the bed, dangling his big black medicine. "It's going to pinch a little bit."

"Hold on," I said, and gripped my head, and tried to hold the vertigo inside. "Just wait a minute, please."

"Is it the spinning?" asked The Sludge. "Come here, I'll cup your head until it stops."

The Sludge anticipated needs. He was my nurse and guardian. He said, "I'm not here for an instant fix. I want to prove I've changed," and he was patient with my hesitation. I thought that we — the perpetrator and the victim — had made our peace. We had been cleansed. I thought about the poseur theologians seeing *that*. How dare they judge me when I didn't castigate but I absolved my enemy. "Come here, my little chickpea, have your water and your pills," he sang to me, and held my head up while I drank. "Good girl. Let's get you fixed."

Then suddenly, as trees began to sacrifice their leaves and point their hoary fingernails, the days had grown more overcast — at least a month of cloudy days with very little sun. The Sludge fell into some kind of depression then. He sighed with frequency, his giant shoulders slumping down. He didn't feel like cooking for me, and he stared out at the street. His tone abruptly changed. He often snapped at me, or just seemed gone. "I'm seasonally malcontent," he said, and sighed. "That's all."

"I need you to be present," I said to The Sludge, who had a name, and I'd begun to call him that. I knew the power of nomenclature, and I finally trusted him enough to call him by his proper name. "I need you with me, Speck."

"But why?"

"I need to know you're really with me, really here."

"I don't know why you care."

He wanted me to say I did, I cared.

The more he wanted it, the more I couldn't say it. He withdrew and part of me expanded. When I thought that he was giving in to his own melancholy, all my anger toward him swelled. I thought about the life I could have lived, the one without an injured brain and sagging bed. The weaker and more desolate he looked, the more I grieved the losses he had caused. The first year I was sick, I thought that all the nonsense of my health would end. No *way* could I be sick another month. I was a girl trapped in an orphanage who always packed her bags and stared down driveways, sure that I was better than the others in my ward. I was at least a little prettier, or more talented, and would be shuttled back to wholeness soon. The longer I stayed sick, the less I felt that I was blessed. Now it had been three years since I had been disabled by the landslide that had started in my poisoned brain and struck my macrophages, glands, and ventricles. The Sludge could not undo the thing that glued our lives together. So suddenly, as I accepted that he would not rescue me and he accepted what he'd done, we turned into a set of heckling conjoined twins. We had annoying spats.

"You might resent being indentured, but you came on your own terms," I said. "You owe me this. We both know that."

"I know," he said, and sighed. "But sometimes you could show a little gratitude."

The sun had been a fugitive for so long we had stopped our search for it. One afternoon, he lay back on my bed. His omnipresent ornament was fastened to his lower hood. It was his favorite one—a skin-toned cock he bought after he met me.

"Why won't you ever suck it?" asked The Sludge.

"I think it's obvious why not."

"Can you not open up your heart and let this go?" He was exasperated. "Your mouth would be so pretty on my cock."

"It's not just that," I said. "It's that you never used to

make me feel like I was lacking, that I didn't give."

"Well, sure, but I have needs. I just don't always tell you, since I know that you can't fill them. But it never rained this many days in sequence. I'm possessed with gloom."

"Okay then, Speck," I said, and opened up my mouth. "You're on. Gag order this."

It started playfully enough. We wrestled on the bed. The Sludge was sliding it into my mouth. I liked it. Yes, admittedly, I did. I hadn't sucked like that since Jack. I whimpered as he thrust it in. He was right: I had to give him something. It felt good to give. But then, in my own mind, I suddenly was drowning. I felt like I was being bullied underwater, head held down. They say that drowning is an awful way to die, but there are ways to drown—with fluid filling up the lungs—while still on land. The Sludge was rocking back and forth into my throat. He made mechanical grunt sounds. I usually took whatever people gave. But I was pushing out, not taking in. I couldn't signal him to stop. I grappled with my hands and tried to shove The Sludge away. Caught in a motion, he did not respond until I punched him in the gut. I sunk into the dough of him. He rolled away from me, the stiff cock pulling from my mouth. I only cared about my breath. "I couldn't breathe," I gasped. "I can't."

He held his gut and looked at me in shock. I'd never laid a hand on him before. His eyes turned into coils of rattlesnakes. I must have punched him hard. I angled slowly toward the wall. He rubbed his belly where my fist had hit. I knew I didn't have the strength to really hurt him. He was muscular, and tall. "Are you okay?" I asked.

"I'll get your oxygen," he said, his speech completely desiccated. He left for longer than was necessary, then he wheeled the tank in and put it six feet from the bed. His eyes were blank as tacks. I was exhausted and my muscles hurt so much I couldn't move. He knew that fucking, even talking, wore me out. He always brought the tank, but typically, he wheeled it close so I could turn the valve, so I could fix the tube around my ears and nose.

"I can't get up," I said. His face was making me uneasy. I tried to sound as sweet as possible, as if negotiating with a rabid dog. "I'm too sick to get up. Speck, honey? Could you just hand me the tube?"

He stood still for a minute, deadpan, looking for the hidden girders that had landed on my bones. He pulled his jeans on, and his boots, but kept his arms crossed over his unbuttoned shirt. In his eyes, I saw the flicker of disgust. I felt revulsion washing over me, directed at my ashy flesh and sallow eyes. I was negotiating with a tentative Morse code of blinks. But suddenly, he charged up to the bed. He grabbed my shoulder, and he heaved me to the floor. "You fucking bitch," he yelled.

My body thudded on the ground before I could react. He kicked me in the chest, then in the ribs. I tried to shuffle backward, but he moved too fast. And when I tried to look at him, to plead for him to stop, he seemed to think a moment then he kicked me in the face.

"Get it yourself," he said, then added, "cripple."

I heard his stomping boots, the slamming door. The interruption, then continuation on the other side.

The room felt like it had been drained of air.

The air was being slowly rationed from the end of a balloon. I lay unmoving for a while, then willed myself to stand. My will, for once, was working on my body. I willed my legs to walk. I pressed my ear against the door but didn't hear him moving. I touched my skin all over but I found no blood. Some welts were forming on my chest and near my cheekbone. My skin felt otherworldly. Each time I touched my cheekbone, I could see a flash of light in front of my right eye. I felt my heartbeat splintering inside. It sounded like a spray of bullets on the paper wall that was the outline of my bodice. I had become a pattern of a person then.

My instinct was to walk away from where it happened, as I would have done if I were lying in my own crushed car with broken glass. I thought that if I turned my head, I'd see an X where I had been. The wreckage seemed specific to that place and not to him or me, though when I walked I felt like bones were falling out of me. My bones were in a soggy grocery bag and falling to the ground, and not a thing could be contained, though everything felt calm. I was embarrassed by my naked, leaking bones. It was the kind of scene you would see after a tornado, when one freakish couch sits in a field of pulverized belongings. I looked down at my hand. My skin itself contained an eerie silence. It was an auditorium of Philip Glass after an afternoon of broken glasses.

I paced around the room with cotton in my step, as if enslaved in soft sharp fields. I saw no exit sign. My body stuttered through the room until I finally reached the door. I had no choice but to go out.

The Sludge was crying in the other room when I walked out. I was aware of how the whole room was positioned. Where the door was, where he sat. The distance between A and B and me—the last-ranked C. At first, I thought that he was sitting stoically, but then I noticed he was crying. I felt relief and nausea all at once. "What have I done?" he said, and wiped his eyes. "I hurt you. I am monstrous and insane." He looked to make sure I was listening, and I pretended that I was. My ears, in fact, had filled with bees as soon as he had bruised my ribs. My ears were as cacophonous as beehives on the inside. I had the feeling that I was a ghost, that I was just a pocket of cold air. I wanted to get out of there. I floated past him, and he tried to grab my arm but I pulled back, reflexively.

"What have I done?" he wailed again when I shirked

back. "Oh God. Now you're afraid of me."

I couldn't understand why I did not react except with that one little pull. The old phantasmagoria of my amygdala was gone. I stood there holding everything inside. My rib was throbbing suddenly. I hugged my body with both arms. I didn't really know if I was scared, but when he said I was afraid of him I thought that he would know. The bees were swarming, and their honey slid around the structure of my brain. I took a wheezy breath. I wasn't crying, not like he was doing — whiny little bitch. I knew I'd better speak.

"We'll deal with this," I finally said, as calmly as I could.

He looked at me with plaintive, hopeful eyes. "What did you say?"

"We'll deal with this."

"We will?"

My voice was wispy, and it came from somewhere else. I listened to it through a tape recorder. "Of course we will. It was an aberrant event."

The more I spoke the more I sounded like I had authority. The sounds were right up in my ear. The humming of the fridge was a mosquito that I couldn't bat away. Still, I swatted at my nose as if the sound came from inside of me. I sat down heavily. I sat down next to him. I couldn't think where else to go. Point B was far away, too many paces out. Point A was a magnetic pole. My soggy bag of bones slumped down. I had to fold the monster into me.

"Wasn't it?" I then reiterated, leading him along, though I was losing journalistic objectivity. "An aberrant event?" I thought if we could have a definition, we could be on the same team. We could be angry at the *aberration*, not ourselves.

"Of course it was. I wasn't thinking. And I love you," he said one more time, and fumbled toward me for a hug. "You know that I would never want to hurt you.

ORIGAMI STRIPTEASE

I love that you're so good and understanding."

He pulled my body close to his, then let me go. I felt the way I folded up into Speck's grasp, a geisha's fan. I didn't see a trace of anger in the way he moved. His irises had filled with pity. He wore his funeral eyes. We'd both switched rotely from destruction to small acts of usefulness, as if we knew—had always thought—the dam would overflow. He seemed to know the rag of me beside him meant that he was indispensable. "I'm going to get some ice," he said and bolted up. "So you don't have a shiner on your eye." We both knew we were rallying together then.

He didn't know I'd taken all the ice-cube trays away and thrown them in the trash, when Jack was reenacting frozen hells. I heard him rummaging around. I knew that he was frustrated but keeping his frustration at a hum and not a scream. He had to be my Mr. Fix It. "Where's the ice?" I heard him muttering. I heard the opening and closing of the cabinet doors and, momentarily, I glimpsed the streetlight shining through the tiny window in the door. The light looked insincere and I convinced myself it was. The imitation moon man couldn't tempt me from the house. He came back with a bag of peas.

"You want to hold it?" he asked in his sweetest voice. He gestured with the bag.

"Thank you," I said through my sore jaw, and took the frozen bag. I put it on my aching eye. I gazed—a Cyclops—through my other eye at him, and he looked bigger and distorted, like a funny face seen through a fish eye lens. He'd made a one-eyed monster out of me. It was no longer clear to me which one of us was wrong. I'd punched him first. I angered him. He just reacted, didn't he?

"Roughhousing can get out of hand," he said, as if to understand himself. "A gentle house can turn into a rough house. Things can happen, accidents." He clasped his hands together and he stared at them—a file of evidence.

"They can. Of course." It sounded very sensible. It sounded like a public service billboard.

"You're right," he said. "You're always smart and right. That's why I like you. You're so good. You will be fine. You're tough."

I worked the pulley of my smile and opened up the velvet drapes.

"Let's never fight like that again," he said. He held the bag of peas against my eye. "Why don't you rest your head?" He put a pillow on his lap. His voice was soothing and etheric. "Why don't you just relax?"

He patted everything to make himself as flat as possible. I felt him stretching out my legs. I felt him softening his lap. "Just lie back," he said in his kindest voice, "and let me be your bed."

I must have slept. I heard the sound of clanking pots. The Sludge was working out the lyrics to the Stones' song "Beast of Burden." I woke up knowing that I should avoid the mirrors but otherwise, I had the feeling of erasure, like my sleep had been a steady rain. My limbs were sore, but that was not unusual. The Sludge was cheerful. "Sausages?" he asked. "I bought a waffle iron." He gestured to the countertop. "I didn't get the heart-shaped kind, don't worry. And I got the gold-foil English butter that you like."

"Thank you," I said. His chatter was a comfort, like a white-noise maker blocking out another person's psychotherapy.

"I also bought some arnica to put on that," he said and didn't look at me.

We both knew what he meant by nonspecific "that." I was embarrassed—even without surveying them all— by all the bruises he had left. We both knew what our job was then, to cover and to bury. I'd seen one spot. Where he had kicked my side, the bruise looked like a kind of butterfly I'd watched in San Francisco called the Mission Blue. This was a long time back, when I was traveling cross-country, in my college years. Someone had given me binoculars, and I was using them. This butterfly is one that feeds upon a special kind of lupine, which is only found around that bay. The flowering plant— named for a wolf I'm guessing—is a bruise of blue. The larvae of the Mission Blue need ants to be their caretakers, to keep away their predators and stroke their backs so they can feed the ants with honeydew. That morning, as I saw the first bruise in the mirror, I let the flitting facts of butterflies take me away. I thought about the way my need for Speck had put a fish eye lens on everything. I thought about the way that symbiosis happens everywhere, and those of us who think ourselves the butterflies are often ants. There's nothing more pedantic than a bruise who sees it otherwise.

While he knocked pans around, and I tried hugging in the pain around my ribs, I thought about that trip to San Francisco, when I learned a multitude of ways of being tie-dyed, queer, and open to all definitions, and I wondered if he'd mention what he'd done. My skin bruised easily, and it would take at least two weeks for it to fully sink to pale. I almost dreaded that, my defloration, more than anything. My body was a little too efficient at the task of shuttling evidence away. It wasn't hard for me to stay away from people and from mirrors for two weeks. We ate in silence for a while. He cut into a sausage, and he dipped it in his syrup. Then he piped up suddenly.

"I'll get some medication," said The Sludge. "I think that's what I need. I will take care of this."

"You will?" I was surprised at how proactively he'd spoken.

"Of course. It will be fine." He leaned over and kissed my cheek. "At least I've finally said I love you, right? I'm crazy over you. It hurts me that you don't feel quite the same."

He sounded wistful when he handed me that power. It felt good right then to know that I did not requite his love. I also felt a little guilty. I had him on a leash. And who does not resent a noose that has been prettied up for public eyes?

An age of industry came after that. We told ourselves that we were handling the problem. There were pills and anger management and therapy. We both knew he had been depressed, and sure, some fabric will unravel if you don't quite serge the edge. He saw the doctor in a timely manner. The pills seemed helpful, and they buoyed my sense of hope that yes, some peace could be extracted from that awful day. The Sludge began to look for work. He kept the newsprint in his car because the chemicals in ink began to make me sick. He came home with proud stories of his meetings with executives. "I'll only work part-time," he said. "I told you I'd take care of you. But we could use the extra cash. One day, I'd like to buy a house for us, a cozy Cape."

"We'll both feel better when you find a job," I said in my affected fifties-Thorazine-numbed-housewife-speak. Conservative and sober words began to sound the most insane. "We've both had too much stress at home."

I didn't know how strapped for cash we were because he'd taken over managing our money. I hadn't brought a single dollar in for quite some time. The money was all his. Speck had been semifamous once. He ran a company that wrote the music for young pop stars, Stick Her Shock. It groomed and bred and plucked and waxed their images. Speck shaped the tiny Bonzai trees of taut young bodies, and he had a knack for finding—as they called it—"Talent." "Has the Talent had her morning facial yet?" they'd say. Or, "Has the Talent done her warm-ups?"

Where he had grown up, he once told me cagily,

there had been gangs and knives. There wasn't always food to go around. He had to fight for what he wanted. This background helped him to become a crafty businessman, someone who could fling bills to pay for opulent events. The pop stars had to stay in tiny packages. They could not age too fast. The emphasis on youth was paramount. They had to be continually crushed into suspended time. Speck thrived at keeping them preserved. He *knew* what made a hit with radio and video potential. His songwriters were aging flower children who long ago relinquished lyricism to write jingles and do background scores. These songwriters sat in a sweatshop of pianos and cranked out new catchy tunes. The pop stars lay down on assembly lines where they had horehound sprayed into their vocal chords, and where Brazilian wax was yanked off of their twats.

The little girls were perfect. They were not allowed to grow.

This all had happened in the city of angelic sin, where giant letters grow like palm trees from the sides of hills and Botox-wielding doctors sell suspense in animation. It was common for a person there to see himself as master of a bigger alphabet, as puppeteer of age itself. At least a dozen movie stunts a year had stunted characters who'd fallen from their safety lines and broken bones. It was the city of messiah complex, stolen water, mammary inflation. None of what The Sludge had done was out of context in a place that bent reality around a saline sack.

The end of his career had started like a tiny chink of hail upon a windshield. One of his top stars began to overeat. She started bingeing on Ding Dongs and sour cream and onion chips. She also popped amphetamines. Her face became a dust bowl overnight. And she—her name is unimportant—was the only star who could hit high E over C. The world began to see that her insipid lyrics were a lie. Besides, the trends were changing, and the music industry no longer wanted prepubescent girls. The Sludge, of course, had not predicted all of it would end, and spent his money recklessly. He still had holdings and supported me with those for several months. This monetary comfort had allowed me rest. I had depended on his generosity.

I should have mentioned this, how generous he was, and how I took from him. I took a lot. At times, when I look back, I see the ways in which I *was* ungrateful. He did not know that the ink would poison me like that. It's not like injury from chemicals was front-page news. And yet, he came to me, he took accountability and helped me heal. Should I have been surprised that he lashed out?

"I'm beat," The Sludge said one more time, discouraged after many weeks of looking for a job. He sighed and said, "I'll just schlep boxes in a warehouse if I have to."

It's true that the economy was awful then. The next day, I glanced out, and he was sitting in his car all afternoon, just idling. I felt uneasy witnessing his shame (or, shall I say, foreshadowing). That night, I found him in the bathtub with an empty bottle, and the blue dye from the pills around his mouth. His body was completely still.

"Oh God oh God," I screamed. I dragged his wrinkled leaden flesh onto a towel. I punched him in the heart. "Don't die, don't fucking die on me," I yelled. I called the paramedics on the cordless phone and started CPR. I watched them take his body on the stretcher and I didn't really know what I should feel. I'd wished him dead so many times. My thoughts had warped into a dark telekinesis that had led his hands to childproof caps. He'd done exactly what I'd wanted him to do. And I had saved him then. Not from himself—from *me*.

Something had happened when that killing urge was kindled and he took those pills. Something had happened when the idling turned to action. Besides the fact that I felt guilty and indebted then, Speck also seemed to realize he'd aimed the weapon wrong. We never talked about the reasons why he tried to kill himself that night. I think they were implicit. The Sludge came home despondent from the hospital. He said: "I am a failure. I'm a monster. I am ruin."

"You're not," I said, and patted him. I stroked his head. "You're really not at all."

"I cannot take your numb derision when I almost died," he said.

He swung at me like it was just for sport, just sparring, and he hit me in the chin. I heard my jaw crack and the sound of bones. The sound of bones collapsing under hands.

And then my shattering began.

3.

"This part is awful. You should turn away." Speck cupped his hands over my eyes. He liked to act like he protected me from things. "I am the strong man. I'm the big guy," he would say, and flex his tattooed arms.

On weekends, now that Speck was working at the candy factory, we rented films. He brought home candy rejects from the factory, and I made popcorn. Stale Christmas came each day, as he had many bags of broken candy canes. He hadn't had an "incident" in weeks. He'd rented *Once Were Warriors*. Speck didn't know it was about a batterer, a daughter's suicide, and some Maori people's alcoholic pain.

"I'd kill that guy," he said, and gestured to the screen so that my eyes were freed.

I saw the woman's bruises outfitting her skin. The characters were in New Zealand, a place that was eclipsed as long as we were bathed in light. New Zealand was the night that proved our day, and we were bisected by slatted light between our regulated windows. The violence there was worse, and I had no right to complain.

"You want some popcorn, sweetie?" I asked meekly, holding up the bowl.

"I'm sorry for my anger," said The Sludge. "That guy reminds me of my dad."

He pulled me up against him, and he fed me chunks of chocolate-covered caramel. He smelled like house dust and familiar sweaters. "She should kill that guy," he said and gestured angrily. "That guy's a fucking alcoholic." The Sludge did not drink alcohol, or not with any frequency. He liked to sip a root-beer float. I'd gotten him some special straws, the kind that kids use. They were made of hard twirled plastic, bent in shapes like animal balloons. He pursed his lips around the straw, then offered me a sip. I drank some from the side and got an ice-cream mustache. "Doing ice-cream drag?" he asked, and smiled as if he loved me. Then he took his sleeve and wiped the white away. He paused the video just after they had found the daughter, who had hanged herself.

There was a feeling that I came to recognize, the subtle barometric change before a cyclone hit. I felt it then.

"I want to talk to you a minute. I have been wondering some things," he said. His voice had dropped. He let the glass clink on the coffee table. He took one of my hands and started playing with my knuckle. "You must know you confuse me."

"How?" I asked. The taste of chocolate in my mouth had suddenly turned bitter.

"I have been wondering why you like it rough. At first you're pale and sweet and then you turn into a toreador's cape. Why are you such a pain slut all the time?" He sanded down my knucklebones. He liked to rub the places where my bones were obvious and pushing out.

"When do you mean? What are you asking me?"

"You heard me. When you're getting fucked. Why do you always want it hard? Why do you make your butches give it to you hard? You told me that you liked it hard with Jack. You always make me give it to you harder every time."

I took a breath. The Sludge had made it clear that he thought Jack had treated me like dirt, but he was fascinated by our sex life and would ask me lewd and graphic questions. Sometimes, he would just say, "I know you'd rather be with him. That hurts me," and he'd pout and act unreasonably wounded. I no longer intoned Jack's name. "I like it soft sometimes," I said. I felt my voice get meek. I reached for the remote to try and turn the movie on again, but when I raised my hand with it, his disapproving glare said it was not polite to point.

"Well, it confuses me and that's not fair," he said.

PEGGY MUNSON

"Sometimes, I think you want—" He twisted up his face with pain.

"What do you think I want?" I asked. I knew where he was going but I couldn't help but egg him on. I wanted him to tell me that I asked for it.

"I wish you'd stop provoking me, that's all," he said. "Sometimes I think you make me out to be the bad guy, and I'm not. You know I'm good to you. I only want to help you and take care of you. Sometimes you really push the pins into the doll."

"I don't mean to push pins."

"Enough of this," he said, and gestured to the screen. "This movie's sad. This kind of tragic human rubbernecking makes me want to fuck." His eyes turned slowly to my lower half.

He took his hand and slid it past my door of clothes. I gasped to feel him touching me. We had not fucked since he had made his suicide attempt. His fingers, on the tips, felt crusty. He slid one in my hole. He had been practicing guitar and building up his calluses again. He bent his head and whispered in my ear. "You know nobody makes me hard like you." He took my hand and made it feel his bulge. I hadn't noticed he was packing, but the evidence was there. He started sliding one rough thumb inside my ass. "You know that you not wanting me just makes me want to die."

I tried to say it gently. "Can you not put it in my ass right now?" I asked. My voice was barely held together in its gelatin. "I don't want sex."

"It's not as if your little sphincter's such a Sphinx," he said. "You're pretty used up, darling."

"I'm just a little sore today."

"My cock is sore and guess who wins."

He pinned my face down on the couch. I heard his belt loops sighing as his belt was freed. I felt him pushing up my skirt and pulling off my panties. "I'm going to fuck you here," he said, "and then I'm going to take you

120

to the cemetery."

"Why there?" I tried to act like he was someone else. He wasn't using any lube. He acted mad at how my ass resisted. He was pushing fingers up inside of me to try and open it so that his cock could find its way. At least he wasn't looking at my face.

"Because your other boyfriend fucked you there. God, you're so tight. You're awfully fucking tight. You trying to break my cock in two?"

I laughed to make him soften up and stop. "I'm not," I said. I tried to pull away. I saw his silver watch and thought of pie tins put in windows to keep silly birds from flying kamikaze into them.

His voice got harsh. "Well if you are, I can get one of metal," said The Sludge. "I can get one that's spiky as a mace." He grunted as he pushed it in. My body slid away from him. "Stay still," he said, and held me firm. "Stop messing with me."

"I'm not trying to move."

He put one arm beneath my neck and pulled it up to choke me. "Well you should learn to be a better baby girl. Just squeeze your ass around my cock. Come on, I want to feel your slutty used back door get tight."

My voice was at a whisper. "This isn't what I want right now," I said. I wasn't playing. Then he choked my breath right out of me. He started forcing his way in my ass.

"Well good," he said. "Because I'm sick of how you talk of Jack—like he's a Sistine Chapel painting. You hurt me and you know it. I'm being shoved into the dirt by an ungrateful bitch. How does this feel?"

"It hurts," I said, when he released my breath.

"That's good," he said. "Because I don't want my girl sitting pretty. I don't want my girl sitting and complacent all the time."

The rape was not much longer than a song. He stopped

and pulled me up to stand. He looked at me as if he could not quite remember who I was. I stumbled and I fell right into him. I was so weak. "It's time to dance with skeletons, so move your bones around the room. I want you to wear Daria's pink dress," he said.

I knew the girl that he was speaking of. Her name was pronounced *dare-e-uh*. They called her "Dare." They paired her sometimes with a girl named Ruth and billed them Ruth or Dare when they were touring Russia, Yugoslavia, or France. The dress was Speck's most coveted possession. He kept it on a special peg. At first he told me Daria had given it to him, but then he said he'd "given her a sweet sixteen" to trade her for the dress.

"What does that mean?" I asked.

"I put a fast car in her driveway," bragged The Sludge. "I put my motor vehicle in her garage."

He didn't tell me straight out what he'd done, but Daria's the one who started eating, his most special pop-star girl, and over time I figured out that he was fucking her. The dress was way too small for me but it was made of stretchy lace so I could make it work. My body could be forced.

"You know that if you rip it I'll be very mad," he said. I sucked my stomach in. I tried to be as pulled inside as I could be. "Mind over flab," my mother used to say. We looked at pastries and resisted. "Conscious liposuction" was our term. Daria was only seventeen when she was fired, exactly half my age. Just recently, I'd figured out that they were still in touch, although I'd turned the other way when I found notes he'd written her addressed to "little superstar."

He said, "Now maybe you will stop pretending you're the cock in this relationship. You act like you're hung like a punching bag."

A guillotine of chill came down. I had the vertigo again; it felt as if my head was spinning off of me. I tried to think of something as compact as grammar, word use, time. I thought, *the word is hanged, not hung.* The girl on TV *hanged* herself. Or was it *hung?* I hung the jury every time I tried to reason out a simple thing. The girl who hanged herself, was she hung like a punching bag? Did she just think she was? At home, there was no question who was hung. My hangman was more hung. The hard hung hangman did whatever hate instructed him to do. Each night, he hung the kittens of my sleep and drew a noose around my hope.

The wheels peeled off the still-damp streets, but all the rain had stopped. "I want to know exactly where he did it," said The Sludge. He pulled over the car when I said stop. I couldn't show him where Jack fucked me, so I led him right past Freelove's headstone all the way to one etched with the name "Narcissa Snow." "That's perfect for a Snow White narcissist like you," he said. He reached into his pocket, and he drew out a knife. I started looking for a place that I could run, but life could not win head counts there. The place was owned by death. The markers were like pages at the end of books that said The End The End The End.

His voice was sweet as children's cough syrup. "I'll just break skin," he said. "I won't cut off your clitoris, you egotist. Turn off your rabbit eyes."

"I'll give you anything you want," I begged. "But please, I don't like blood." I tried to back away, but I could barely separate my legs. I'm sure it looked comedic, how the sausage casing of the dress constricted me.

"Right now you're just so pink," he said. "That dress. I think red is more definite, don't you? The pink is straddling the fence. The pink is love me, love me not. The pink is noncommittal. Pink is you. I want you to be red. I want you to be flaming hot for me. I want you to be definite."

"I'm serious," I said. "Just stop. You're talking crazy,

and it's scaring me."

"Come on, just play along with me." He turned on his charisma and his Manson eyes. "Let's think about the things that start with pink. First, we have pinking shears. I like the way serrated lines look like the mouths of dead cartoon characters. Then there's 'in the pink.' The place you go after a long productive convalescence. The place you go when leeches bleed you out. Which do you choose? Are you a dead cartoon or someone bleeding back to life? What will it be, pink dress? Should I cut out your cartoon mouth with pinking shears? Do you want to be bled to health?"

"That's kind of—what's it called? A Hobson's choice." I felt like I was going to cry but held it in. He stroked the blade. It was insane how sane he looked when doing it.

"Two choices, sweetheart, and you've got one chance to answer here. Are you a line drawing or not? Are you a set of pinking shears? Are you a zigzag Lombard Street? Or not?"

I didn't understand The Sludge's crazy questions, but I answered anyway. "I'm not a line drawing. I want to choose the one that's not cartoon."

"Good girl," The Sludge said. "And what makes humans different from cartoons? Our blood and only that. So why don't you stop giving lip? Should I just cut your pretty mouth to make a gorge for all your chattering?"

"Don't cut my face," I said. "Just do it anywhere but there."

"So then you're ready to stop being pink?"

"I am," I said.

"Then say it in a sentence."

"I don't want to be so...pink."

"Then say you love me more than Jack. Say something real. Stop hurting me." He sounded genuinely anguished.

ORIGAMI STRIPTEASE

"I love you," I said, lying to his face. "I love you more than Jack. Believe me, Speck, I do."

He put his lips up to my mouth. His breath was awful, like it had been locked inside a moldy room. "I'm going to make you know you do," he said.

I felt the tug of fabric on my hip. I looked down and I saw he'd slid the knife beneath the fabric and he'd cut it, just one cut to free my skin. "Well look how white you are," he said. "Your flawless gesso skin." Without a moment's thought, he started writing on my skin with the blade as calmly as a person writing with a pen. "Let's see," he said. "I might need help in spelling. You'd better call out letters since I'm just a stupid thug. We'll start with something obvious. Spell 'whore' for me?"

He made me spell it out. He carved those letters into me, in shallow tiny script above my pubic bone. "The *W* I cut looks like a flying pelican," he said. "But don't pretend it is. Don't you feel flightless anyway?"

He propped me up against the headstone with my beading blood around the word. I was a signpost. I felt faint. I slid down like a ragdoll, landing with my butt upon the muddy ground. He shook my head and looked at my pathetic sinking skeleton. "I'll bet she'll be real mad when she sees how you desecrated that," he said, and clucked his tongue.

"Who will be mad?" I asked. My head felt like a helium balloon.

"Why, Daria," he said. "She will be *furious*. I called her earlier. I asked her truth or dare, and she went for her namesake right away."

That's when I noticed Daria was sitting in a tree with dark bush-baby eyes and slicked-back hair. She pursed her vapid little lips then hopped the four feet to the ground.

"You ready to be raped?" The Sludge asked, smirking at the girl.

"Of course," she said, conspiratorially. The curves

looked good on her. She looked much better than she did in her lean years. She also had a new sophistication with her shorter hair. "You know I love it when you rape me, boss."

"You're much better at being good than her," he said, and gestured at my unnamed face.

"That's 'cause she's bloody old," said Daria. "And bloody. Gross. She is a walking maxi pad."

"That might be true if she would ever end her record-breaking PMS. She thinks that I abuse her," said The Sludge, although I had not said those words. "She's whiny, Daria. She can't take it as good as you."

"That's why you hired me, boss. Remember? I'm a star."

"I'll tell you what. Let's do a tombstone rubbing then. Your cute posterior up in the air. Once for posterity?"

"Of course!"

They did it garishly. I watched him fuck her on the stone and shake the fake cum off his dick. I saw it all—his biggest cock, her body tottering. She made exaggerated squeals for me, so I would know right when she came. "That was a high O over C," she said, and giggled when the deed was done, amused by every sound her mouth could make. They kissed again and pulled apart reluctantly, like strands of taffy. "I'll miss you, little superstar," he said to her.

"I'll miss *you*, boss," she said.

The Sludge was cheerful afterward. "Somebody shows appreciation," said The Sludge, his big hand resting on the wheel. "Maybe you'll learn a thing or two from little sister." I tried to nod, but I felt devastated. Thankfully, I didn't bleed to death or anything. The dress looked like a doily dipped in blood. "Maybe," I said. "Maybe I'll learn." I felt so miserable that he took pity and his voice turned kind for just a second. He put his big hand on my thigh. "You look like you've been gutted," said The Sludge.

ORIGAMI STRIPTEASE

I nodded aimlessly. I felt light-headed, gone.

"We'll get that washed up when we get back home," he said. "You know that you're my only home. She's chicken and you're steak. It's just that she's hot chicken. Could you see how tight she was?"

I shook my head. I stared at all the people walking by, the lonesome puppetry.

"Well, take my word," he said. When we got home, he didn't hit me, but I almost wished he would. I wanted full-on contact.

"What's black and white and crusty brownish-red all over?" asked The Sludge. He dabbed a washcloth on the wound.

I shook my head.

"Old news," he said. "Or you."

4.

The unkind casing of my flesh was suddenly much better than the domicile I shared with Speck. I studied architecture from the ground. I gave the hardwood floors their name. Sometimes, as I was walking by, he stuck a leg out, and he made me trip. This might seem odd, but when I stumbled to my room and took the journal out, I often wrote about the molding or the walls or doors.

Take, for one, the lowly door, an instrument that I considered daily.

A door seems simple when you're not inside a house, when not ensconced in all the hidden wallpaper of noise. There is the wallpaper outside the mind — the thermal mass that sponges up the anger and the makeup sex (you give yourself to him, because your bones are taken care of then). Then there's the wallpaper within, the thin veneer of cardboard that becomes your home when you are being hit. In fact, the skull becomes a reed, and all things passing through make sound. You hear the shouting, but the words are nonspecific. You listen for a riptide in the tone. A big shark champing at your arm would be too obvious. It's not like that. It doesn't feel like that. It feels like something sucking underneath, and you go willingly, because you know that fighting only makes the wave more eloquent and powerful. You are a needle coursing through a thick and batted piece of cloth, and you just wait to reach the eye of light that is your own, your trailing eye.

The door is also just like you. It opens when it's touched and tries not to become unhinged. You start to hate its small, pathetic stillness. The door reminds you just how weak you are. If you were strong you'd simply leave. You know that you are waiting, but you're not sure why. Perhaps you're looking forward to the moment when your suffering is turned around? The door is

waiting to expose its inverse too. You both wait patient-
ly for that. The underbelly. Yet you wonder what is incu-
bating everywhere—what danger and what pain. The
door is nothing but a tocking block of wood, a small percussive taunt. It leads you to another room where you
are quick to see the sunset get beheaded by the edge of
your escape route. A door seems simple when, once
breaching it, you can break out and run. Imagine if,
instead, you had a rock tied to your ankles and nobody
but the demon could take it away.

You'd have no place to go, or would you now?

One time I took the car, and thought I'd get away.

I thought I'd drive so fast I'd break the sound and
kinesthetic barriers. I took the car to where, two days
before, I'd seen a fox. The day I saw the fox, The Sludge
had taken me with him to get the groceries. The fox was
scurrying across a busy city road. At first I thought it was
a dog, but then I saw it had more hubris than a dog. It
didn't know its way around and seemed surprised by
traffic. There were no forests anywhere nearby, and this
was in the busy center. It was near dusk, and I imagined
that the fox had offspring and it probably hunted squir-
rel. It was the only miracle I'd seen in quite some time.
The Sludge was kind enough to slow the car, which
made the fox go in a jagged line. It didn't speed across
the way a rabbit or a panicked deer might do. I didn't
speak a word, but felt my body lightening, and gasped.

The fox came by to tell me that there was another
place. The fox had come for me.

The Sludge had gone out with a buddy on the night I
took the car. The night was misty as the cover of a card.
I pulled the car out slowly, anxiously, as if the neighbors
would report me for escaping him. The windows were
fogged up. I was afraid that I would hit a person walking by the road, and then my troubles would compound.

PEGGY MUNSON

I didn't pack my stuff because I thought The Sludge would spring to action faster then, and he might come and find me. I thought my headlights must be out, as I could not detect if they were casting light and cars kept driving out in front of me. The visibility was very low that night. That's why a car ahead of mine had hit the fox. I didn't see the impact, but I saw the lump and swerved around, as other cars were doing. Then I circled back to try and see if it was still alive. When I looped back around the boulevard, I noticed that a car behind me pulled aside and put its blinkers on. I circled back and saw that car was sitting there. I squinted for the lump but didn't see it then.

I thought the fox had gotten up and limped away. I thought, I hoped, that it was not quite dead, just maybe shocked and wounded, hobbling off. But then I saw its folded body on the grass. Someone had dragged it over there. It was contorted strangely, and its bushy tail was curled around its side. Its head was bluish gray and beautiful, flat on the dewy green. I steered my car to where it was. I didn't see a drop of blood, but I knew that the fox was dead. I got out of the car. "Oh, God, I'm sorry. You did nothing wrong," I said. The hope inside of me was crushed. The car with blinkers must have been the one. I'm sure the driver thought at first—since he'd been ambushed—that he hit a dog. A lot of people walk their dogs along the boulevard. Would he have pulled aside to help the animal if he had known that it was just a measly fox? Did he just slalom through his rods and cones instead of seeing what was there?

The road was long and treacherous ahead. It was the kind of night when poets punch the magic from a fairy tale of gingerbread by sticking their heads into the gas. An outsider could not survive two days outside a habitat—was that the moral here? I suddenly felt panicked and alone. When I drove home, and opened up the door, my sad life greeted me, an inconclusive parable. The fox had stumbled into my interior; now he was gone. I was alone, and there were formless lumps of horror in my dreams, a spew of carrion, the parts of me that scattered bloody everywhere.

Speck rattled through the flimsy door at one.

"It's good I didn't drink so that I could drive Zero home," he said when he returned. "It is a wicked broth out there. Girls were auditioning to be a welded ornament upon the hood. I couldn't see my hands."

"Maybe you have no hands," I said.

"Nobody said that you could make a wish," he said, and slapped me on the ass.

5.

I watched the house and how it swayed, did not protect. The house was stoned and inattentive on the evening that he stole my journal from its drawer. By stoned, I mean, the house was beaten dead by rocks. The house was battered, bloody as a victim of religious persecution. The house was also higher than my parents at a Jimi Hendrix concert, jacked up from the ground.

The smoke, which made me sick, was wafting underneath my bedroom door. The Sludge had his buddies over. Brother Zero, Carny Tom, The Wrench. I heard them laughing in the other room. I heard the doorbell ring. I smelled the pizza. They were watching porn again. They loved the basest grunt-and-fuck pornography. I heard the women squealing and exclaiming "Yes, oh yes, oh baby, yes." Everything was funny to the boys when they were high. Oh, God, it was so fucking funny. The smoke died down and they had mellowed to philosophizing. I heard their existential whispers and their chortles.

"Where's your wife?" I heard Tom say.

My eyes went to the threshold of the wooden floor. I barely had a moment to feel dread before The Sludge stomped in my room and dragged me out. He sat me down beside him, and he kissed my cheek. "I love this pretty paper doll," he said to them, and I could almost see the *Awwww* flash in their eyes. I saw how they were floating through a scrolling lake of sky. The Sludge looked at me like he had just realized I wasn't real. He started peeling off my flesh in front of them for rolling paper, and he rolled a joint. My God, it was so fucking funny, how he ripped me into pieces and they watched.

Revise that: no, he wasn't peeling off my flesh but he was doing worse. He was caressing me and telling me my skin felt soft. He wasn't stopping them from hazing

132

ORIGAMI STRIPTEASE

me. I didn't realize I had been thrust on stage. Somehow, The Wrench had found my journal and was reading it aloud. He found a page in which I'd drawn a picture of a swan. "The title of today's selection is 'The Swan,'" he started reading, mockingly. Their eyes were like those lightning bulbs that make a zigzag flash to any point a finger touches on the glass. Their pupils were like tumors. Everything reeked of the putrid-sweet of marijuana smoke. There was the tense containment of a high that felt, ironically, like something plunging toward metastasis. "'The Sludge and I went for a drive today,'" he read. "Hey man, she calls you Sludge. No pet names here." The boys all chortled gaily.

"Please do continue," said The Sludge, whose voice had suddenly turned professorial.

"'I hadn't left the house in weeks. I felt like shit. It was a sunny day,'" he read.

"Does this get interesting?" piped Brother Zero (nullifying loser like his name). "I can't take someone's sentimental, poorly written journal."

"No kidding," added Tom. "If I want Disney when I'm baked, I rent *Fantasia*."

"Wait, there's more," said The Sludge. "Relax." He squeezed my arm.

"Ahem. She writes: 'We parked beside the river. All the factories were dormant, standing spindly, lost, like locust skins blown over to the other side. The Sludge spit out a plague of nothingness as he sat next to me. I would have rather just been tortured in a way that was more obvious than his indifference. The Sludge was sullen and his attitude was tainting everything. I hadn't had an outing in three weeks! He didn't seem to care or want me to have fun. He stared ahead, and I looked out the parked car window at the riverbank. I counted beer bottles and condom wrappers there. He had the most retracted eyes. I hated him.'"

The Wrench let out a gasp. "She's traitorous," he

said. "You hear that, man? 'I hated him'—what's that about?"

"I heard," said The Sludge. He rolled his bloodshot eyes. "Get out the violins."

"Go doubt the violence?" said Tom. He was too high to hear.

"I'd leave the bitch for writing that," The Wrench whispered, then he took a swig of beer. "Christ, you do everything for her."

The Wrench continued. "'Suddenly, through all the edging plants, a swan appeared. It was not six feet from the car. I gasped. "A swan!" I said. I couldn't help but talk out loud. I thought inside that some totemic act of beauty always comes in times like this, in times when you lose faith and start to fill with hate. "Look, Speck, a swan!" I said, with glee. He turned his stupid head my way and looked. He seemed perturbed that he was inter-rupted. He took a swig of root beer. "Swans are mean," was all he said.'"

"What is that poem in which the god becomes a swan and rapes a girl?" asked Tom.

"It's Leda," said The Sludge. "It's 'Leda and the Swan.' The William Butler Yeats poem written from the myth of Leda. Please do go on." He gestured to The Wrench.

"'So then we fought. "How can you say that swans are mean?" I yelled at him. "They are," The Sludge said, and shrugged. "They are aggressive. Everyone knows that." He was so smug and patronizing. "That's not the point," I cried. "The point is that I haven't left the house in twenty days. The point is that a flash of beauty came upon my car, and you just poison everything. You never let something be pure. It always has to wear your stamp of negativity." Later, when I told my friend, she said, "Sure, swans are mean. They're mean like people with extraordinary beauty." Speck would never say some-thing so poetic.'"

"That's heavy," said The Wrench. He raised his roach. "But man, can I just say: this shit is good. This buzz is like a vibrator against a doorknob. My head is humming."

"It's true. This shit you brought today is good," The Sludge then seconded approvingly, and raised the bag of weed to wave at Brother Zero.

"Thanks," Brother Zero said. "I had to fuck a fat Hawaiian chick to get this stuff. Five finger squeeze." He formed his hand into a fist.

"Can we sum up this tragicomedy? What happened with the swan?" said Carny Tom.

The Sludge began to paraphrase. "I told her, 'Why don't you go feed the swan if it's so nice?'" The Sludge said, laughing. "She said, 'I'm afraid. Now I'm afraid of swans because of you.' She was so mad at me. So I got out and tossed her sandwich to the swan. The pecker neck devoured the thing in front of her, and viciously. She sulked the whole way home and screamed, 'You're mean. You are the one who's mean.' She couldn't recognize the way the swan lunged for my hand and almost took it off. Some people are attached to their illusions."

"Fuck you," I said.

"Say what?" The Sludge's eyes were glazed.

"You heard me. Fuck you all," I said. I got up and I started stomping out of there.

I heard Tom say. "That girl's a drama queen. She needs to mellow out."

"Some people are attached to their illusions," said The Wrench, and punctuated with his joint. "Now that's a fucking poem, my friend."

I put a towel under my door to keep the smoke away, but it was seeping in all night.

6.

There were the times I cut myself, just two. The razor blade was easy on my skin, so fast, the blood responding quicker than a paramedic does. I realized why someone might become a cutting hobbyist. Had I been standing on the ladder of another person's happiness back when I thought that I was generating goodwill on my own?

Sometimes, I wanted every blade to fall, so that I didn't have to wait. I wanted him to pummel me so I could feel the end, instead of being trapped within the barometric plunge. There were unquiet stretches when he didn't grab my hair or shout. Sometimes, I "took my medicine," as old folks used to say, and he hit hard, but usually not. My medicine was but a part of my panoply of pain. His fist inoculated me against his shouts. The noise collected in the room like unspayed cats who bred and mewed incessantly. I was a person overrun in my own house, and it was too embarrassing to voice how out of hand things got. He always let me know the world was past my reach, and I could not survive without his help. This fact was real. I'd gotten sicker as the months wore on. I needed him to bring me water in my bed. Some nights he helped me up to pee. I couldn't walk the journey—even to be rid of my own waste—alone.

So how could I be rid of something so immense? I thought of killing him. I thought about it when he slept beside me, weighty as a bag of dimes. But then I came up with so many prohibitions, such as how I couldn't lift his lifeless body to the trunk. Sometimes, just as I might have pictured someone naked to curb fear, I pictured him in concrete shoes. He was already my cement; my ankles were already tied. I thought of poison, knives. I mostly thought of pills, how I could make it look like he had tried to kill himself again. I wondered how to make him swallow, if it were like dogs, the way you have to hold their jaws shut and massage their throats until you feel the reflex kicking in. I knew he would die like a fly on flypaper—not fast at all, but slow and struggling. I couldn't do to him what he had done to me.

I wanted him to die of fear. I wanted him to die a psychogenic death. I wanted for his heart to blow up full of chemicals, the chemicals of fear, and crash into itself. I knew that, metaphorically, that's what he'd done to me.

My murderous imagination rubbed upon a washboard but could not get clean. Some days, a truth serum infused throughout the room. I figured, what the hell, he'd kill me anyway, and opened up my stupid mouth.

"The fox is dead," I said, and bit the sandwich he had made. The bread was that deceptive bread that looks so crispy it is chewy. Everything had grown more rubbery around the house. I was adept at bouncing off.

"What fox?" he asked. His hands were as controlled as watches, moving food around. He was distracted by the task of sorting lettuce leaves.

"The one we saw when we were driving to the store. It's dead." I talked while I was chewing, gnashing out my words.

"How do you know it's *dead?*" We were competing with that word.

"I took a drive one night." I said it like it was an everyday event. I liked the way the words rolled out of me.

He turned his hips and slowly rotated his trunk. "When I was out?"

"When you were at the bar with Brother Zero." I checkmated his eyes.

He gave me a queer smile, like he was watching movies of another day behind his eyes. He liked that I was playing cat and mouse with him. It made his task a little easier. He usually didn't have the time to really think about my punishments. My provocation gave him rationale to dole out punches any way he chose. We knew that it was wrong for me to leave. I hoped that he would do it right away, just take me out. The word that day was "dead." I wished he'd saw my rotted trunk and fell my stupid skyward limbs and watch me fall. *Go on,* I thought, *just finish off the job.*

"But wait," he said instead. "I don't recall a fox."

He could have punched me and I would have taken it, and yet, I wasn't going to let him say there was no fox. I wasn't going to stand for this reductionism of a living thing. "Come on," I said. My voice was peevish. "We saw it together. Don't pretend that you weren't there." I rose in pitch to almost histrionic.

"No, no," he said, then did a costume change into his gentle voice, and put one hand upon my forearm. "I mean that it was not a fox we saw. You're wrong." He looked at me like one would look at someone with dementia.

"You're going to claim it was a dog?" I felt like I might cry. I didn't want to talk semantics then. I knew what I had seen.

"I don't deny we saw something unusual that day. But I can see it clear as ice. That beast was bigger than a fox. It must have been a sixty-pounder. I'm sure you noticed that. The thing we saw was a coyote, not a fox. You shouldn't jump to labels if you just don't know. You're always naming names. You think you know the etymology of lisps and stutters too." He took out the serrated knife and started cutting a tomato. He turned the knob and fired the stove. He gaslit me again.

"That's crazy though. I've seen coyotes, and they're small and shy. I've heard them in the woods. I've seen them on clay pots." My voice was shrinking back. I watched him work the knife and red. He saw I empathized, I thought I was a fox.

"In most parts of the country, yes. But here, coyotes grow to sixty pounds, or seventy. And some can fraternize with dogs. They're common here, like rats. We call them *coydogs* here, the ones who breed with dogs. Why don't you know this?" Red was oozing out around his hands. "It's something everybody knows."

"Because it makes no sense. Why would a feral animal have sex with a domestic pet? It seems to me that it would eat the dog."

I thought about the night I saw the lump, how I had first pulled over just to check my headlights since the other cars were acting like I was an umbra. I walked around my car and saw my transportation staring back at me. My car looked charged to go. And no, the wilds of pistons and of fuel did not attack me then. They were not vicious beasts. They welcomed me. They shouldered me and gave me powers that I didn't have myself. The car had made me larger than myself. It hadn't run me down but built me up. It was a night of joinery, of twos, and those who ventured out alone were swiftly killed. The pairs were made in most unlikely ways.

"If you think life's all Noah's Ark and good and bad and pairs of mourning doves, you'll have a rude awakening," he said. "What happened to the dead coyote, anyway?"

He swerved around the lump of truth, that I had disobeyed the tacit fact of my imprisonment. *Or maybe*, I thought cautiously, *I had obeyed by testing out my faith, and reaffirming that I would come back to him*. For doesn't every doctrine have its tests? That night of misty rain had not become a flood, and nothing was premeditated. I hadn't planned to leave; I did come back. The lump, my tears, the rain were trials I passed. I came back to his lair. I proved our shared devotion.

He said: "You are my little coydog, aren't you? My little coy girl sneaking out. My naughty coydog." He waggled one strong finger at my face.

"Sure," I said. I tried to smile. He gave me hypocorisms, but they were always names of hybrids, never cuddly things. His pet names felt more satyr-like than flattery. They didn't let me separate my flesh. I looked out to the empty street. The driveway was a swollen tongue. "Somebody dragged the dead coyote to the side," I said.

"He must've thought it was a dog. He could have gotten rabies. You didn't touch it did you, babe?"

"Of course not, I'm not stupid. I know not to touch a thing like that. The point I'm trying to make was that it made me sad. This is my point. That it was senseless and it made me sad." I wanted him to see that I was human, that I felt. He slowly turned around.

"Well, there are other points to make. Like you, you'd trade a loyal wolf so you could fraternize with dogs," he said. "You would do that to me."

He started laughing, and his head looked like it might fall off. I watched the seam of everything split open. I saw his awful hand around the handle of the cast-iron pan, his sandwich oozing open in the middle. I thought that I should go find Jack. It seemed a logical solution suddenly. I had been living all this time as Jack imagined he was living—trapped in ice. I grabbed what was in front of me and stood and walked a line straight for the door. I wasn't thinking anything, much like the dumb coyote. I was only thinking how to get across, and musing I had never seen a moon as beautiful as all the rushing lights.

"Where do you think you're going, saffron eyes? You going to fuck your dogs?"

"I'm leaving you," I said to him. I said it flatly as I calmly held my journal and my pen. "I am in love with Jack, not you. You're horrible."

I heard him coming up behind me. Whoosh and stomp.

I must have felt the crack of the pan against my skull, but after that, the world became a vein of coal. I thought of Jack and how he waited for me in a den beyond the edge of green. If I could find the reason why he ran, I might be free.

I saw the floor rise up.

And then I saw the gray coyote running through the door, its teeth bared, rushing by. It lunged right by me but our eyes were a communiqué of cup and string. I watched its limber body leap. It sunk its teeth into The Sludge's throat. The Sludge looked frantic and confused. His hands began to girlie-slap the animal away. I felt the splattering of red and underlying snarl. The rope of throat beneath the gritty vowel. I heard The Sludge's baby screams but cupped my hands over my ears. The walls were sprayed with blood. The jaws of death were shredding him. The jaws of life were pulling me out of the wreckage of our home.

There was one part I couldn't watch. It was the final blow. I heard a sound that was like two hands breaking fistholds of spaghetti. This was The Sludge's ripping throat. His pharynx and his larynx and his feeding tube and glands. The animal came over and he dropped a bloody organ at my feet. It was exactly square. It turned a strange Tiffany blue. I fancied, to the fox, the voice box was a jewelry box. In fact, the fox kneeled just as much as a coyote could and looked expectantly at me.

"Are you proposing marriage to me now?" I asked, and watched it nod.

I held my chest and heaved a giant sigh. I took its paw. We walked through the confetti of white light. And then, we became one, my tortured body and my animal betrothed.

Part 3:
What Made Jack Run

1. Cakewalk

My shoulder felt him first. "The truck is idling in the dark," Jack said. "I'm taking us away."

The room was as mucky as a stirred-up pond. I couldn't talk or scream or move. He put his leather arms beneath my back and knees and lifted me. I leaned my head against his chest. "You're very sleepy, little poppy," Jack said to my hair. I felt like we were in an alien-abduction story. The headlights made me think of oval eyes. "I wanted to keep the cab warmed up," said Jack. Emerging from my downy bed, the air had hit me like a wall of Winter Canada. I seemed to have my coat on but my gloves hung awkwardly, as if I held my hands in fists while I was dressed. I wondered how his heart was holding up as he was lifting me. Perhaps he'd crumble into clots of darkened snow. We had the grace of water physiotherapy, as if my body was no effort in a weightless space.

The gravel crackled in the road like heated popcorn kernels in a pan.

We sneaked up quietly. Their arms were twisted strangely or just broken off. One swing was creaking in the gasp of breeze. Just looking at the metal playground made me cold. Half of the heads were broken. All the eyes were blue. The gentle fabrics were impaled on trees, as if the damage happened long ago. Their plastic skin was muddy or ungodly clean. I stepped out of the cab and walked among them quietly. The school was boarded up. Their boxes and their cheery plastic covers spilled out of the dumpster. One of them had both her legs stuck through the fence, no head. I looked down and my twisted gloves looked like their little plastic hands.

"I put them back together, but they fall apart," Jack said. "You are a girl. Maybe you know the secret to the doll enigma."

PEGGY MUNSON

His face was sad. I turned away from him and staggered toward the boarded school. I couldn't figure out why I was having trouble walking. My legs were trapped in memories of stilted piers and fledgling trees. I neared a boarded door and heard distorted music, like calliope pipes filled with soda water. I turned to Jack, confused. His eyes looked pained. He raised one hand. "Is this one mine or yours?" I asked. "Is this one mine?" He didn't answer so my hands began to pull at boards. The nails creaked as the boards fell down in front of me. I opened up the rusty door and peered into the gym.

There was a penny carnival in session. "A hundred tickets for a dollar," said the sign. There was a game where you could knock down bowling pins with tennis balls. There was a makeshift rubber duck pond; ducks with prizes written on their bottoms floating in a round steel tub. The prize table had little wooden whistles, Chinese finger cuffs, a fuzzy bear. The booths all arced around the center of the gym, and there, there was a giant cakewalk filling up the center circle. People marched around a clock-like round, embossing numbers with their feet. The rusty music played. The cakes were spread out on a table, angel food with pink-dyed frosting, German chocolate cake, the whitest layer cake I'd ever seen. The walking people looked exhausted, faces drawn and tired, just like a battered chain gang or a death march. Their skin was pallid; clothes were not so bright. The people from the booths had drifted over. The spectators engaged the walking herd, cajoling, waving arms.

Jack said, "I don't think you should watch."

He tried to pull me back. His hands went over my eyes. I clipped his fingers off of me. The music twirled around the turntable as people walked, their footfalls growing more and more monotonous. The more the people clomped their feet, the better all the cakes looked to my hungry eyes. The bundt cakes drizzled with a cape of

ORIGAMI STRIPTEASE

frosting, cupcakes with a chiseled icing smile on every one. The cake that someone put a wedding bride and groom on top of, for humorous effect—with heads down, not heads up. The music swelled into a dance, a tarantella, so the weary feet sped up their pace. I saw a woman tripping, how her desperate legs could not go on. She caused a pile up. People stepping over her, a trampling. Then the ordinary march until another fell again. Each time a person dropped, the peanut gallery applauded and burst into yokel catcalls. Then they pushed one of their own into the ring. The walk went on all night, the bodies falling into doughy mounds. The cheering was infectious, like the ruckus at a concert. I cheered along with everyone, but Jack stood stone-faced, holding on my arm.

The music grew increasingly aerobic. Half the crowd had fallen down, the bodies shoved aside so we could see the numbers on the ground. There were the boomerangs of elbows pushing new contestants in. The bodies that had fallen crawled away or gave into the crush of stepping legs. The crowd was angling forward. All the cakes looked luscious, drowned in creamy frosting. I felt the push against my back.

"I can't," I said, resisting as my body stumbled toward the walk. "I don't belong with them."

A bearded man was pointing at me with his walking stick.

"She won't," said Jack, and faced the man, who took his stick and whacked Jack to the side.

"She wants to win the cake," the man said angrily to Jack. "She's old enough. Look how she salivates."

And so I finally took my place within the dizzy walk. The human oxen turned the unseen drill. Our hours went by like minutes. No light came in from outside. Bodies fell around me and were trampled into bones. The walking wounded held their arms in phantom slings. The crowd let out a yell that grew in zealousness

147

each time a new contestant fell. They yelled out, "Pussy! Loser! Cheat!" They pelted us with rubber ducks and tennis balls.

As quickly as the guiltless game had grown into a coliseum sport, the music stopped and all the clomping feet stayed on their numbers. The percolating crowd grew quiet. "Hush now. The number will be called," the walking stick man said. He swung his stick and pointed to a lady with a fishbowl full of numbers. We stood like chessmen on our numbers, held our breath. The caller made a pregnant pause. There was an exhalation from her scaly lips. And then she said it, "Thirty-three."

I quickly looked and saw I stood upon the winning number, there with my unworthy shoes. The crowd let out a boisterous cheer. The losers burst into a symphony of cries and wails. Some bookies passed a roll of twenties to a group of winning betters. The cake table was finally wheeled in my direction. I was so hungry for the cakes — I stuck one finger in the pink. I licked the icing from that finger and it was the most delicious pink I'd ever had.

But then the floor began to tremble and the table shook. The ground went Richter. The cake grew bigger, like a yeasty bread put in a sunny place, sextupling in size. It morphed into a bachelor-party cake, the kind a girl jumps out of. All of the other cakes — the chocolate and the pineapple — were pushed aside. "Now dance!" the crowd yelled. "Strip!"

The caller of the number put a piece of chocolate cake into my mouth and said, "You'd better dance. They like to see the winner lose her shirt."

A DJ switched the record to a sultry tune. A church-ly meddler brought a fringed-and-beaded gown to me. I climbed up on a stepping stool and jumped inside the hollowed cake, and then the meddler handed me the costume. The cake was gooey on the inside, where I took my clothing off. I heard the muted voices growing more and more demanding. The cake was rocking back and forth between their warring fronts. I couldn't get my legs through the bikini briefs because I had to hold the sticky walls for balance. The record skipped as it was bumped against and then resumed. I tried to put the string bikini top over my breasts but then I heard an awful rumbling and before I knew it, bits of cake were falling in my eyes and mouth. The sticky frosting was collapsing on my body. The stick spread everywhere. The crowd of people piled on top of me, their tongues and hands trying to eat the cake off my body. Naked in the sticky sweet, I tried to break away. I struggled from a man who licked the frosting from my ear.

As they were mauling me, I felt a tug upon my foot, and all my sugared skin slipped from their hands, and finally Jack was pulling me erect, and we were running from the crowd, who skidded on the frosting mess.

"But wait," I said. "I have to get a cake before I go."

"The cakes are not a prize," said Jack. "The cakes do not come free. The cakes are just another doll enigma."

I wondered why he always thought he could not fix what could be fixed. I knew the dolls had sockets like a simple puzzle, and the cakes looked so rewarding. I needed cake because I'd never been a winner. Jack dragged me as the crowd grabbed frosting from my hair.

He said, "Life's not a cakewalk. All the music starts and ends in slippery want. That's just the way it is."

Photograph: Girls

Month three with Jack.

Jack licked a seam of underwear beside my soft white thigh. He slid an edge of it aside with tongue. His fingers grabbed my hip bones and elastic waist. He pulled my bones to draw me to his tongue. I wished that I could tell him what it was to be a girl: an A-line skirt that was a lampshade lit from broken glass. Jack didn't want to talk. He pulled my underwear and cupped my ass, and watched me kick the panties from my feet. He took his fingers and he gently pried me open. The tiny hairs upon his head were like a lawn—I liked to try and pull what wasn't there. His eyebrows raised as he looked up my skin. "Girls are a language I can only taste," said Jack. "I'm blind like that. You're extrasensory." He slid his tongue straight down my pussy while he put a finger in my ass. He worked his tongue around my clit. "We only make religions out of things we cannot know," he said. With that, Jack opened up the Braille of me and read.

2. Paper

Jack tried to get a station on the dial but there was only static. Any noise, even a noise that sounded like a pan of crackling lard, was better than our breath. The roads had grown into an adolescent scoliosis in our absence. Trees were dangling sleepily beside the road. The stop signs were somnambulists. The headlights were no match against the black. But Jack drove like a man from an asylum, seeking an inviolate unknown. We started up a steady winding incline through the forest but there were no homes, no cars, no signs. As we both looked around for signposts, Jack lost track of where his hands were. And then he almost hit the moose.

His leg went taut against the brake, his body pulling counterweight. I put my hands against the dash and tried to push the motion backward. The friction screeched. We stopped just inches from the moose's massive nose. The moose heaved fog out of his nostrils, staring at our eyes. He seemed nonplussed. His awkward legs and bullish rage faced off against the truck.

"It's not a moose," said Jack. "It is a folding moose."

"Of course it is a moose," I said. "I know a moose, and that's an angry moose."

"That is an origami moose," said Jack. He stepped out of the truck.

"Is this one yours or mine?" I yelled to him. "Is this one yours?"

Jack took his hands and plied one ear back from the moose. Beneath the ear turned up a film of thin red paper with a lotus flower print. He flattened out the moose's head, the moose's nose, the moose's back, until the moose was just a giant sheet of origami paper, lying like a bloodlet road. "Oh, God," said Jack. "I see what's happening." He pulled the bumper off the truck and crumpled it into a paper ball, and threw it to the forest.

"Not that," said Jack. "Not paper everything."

He shook his head. He walked off toward the trees. He took an overhanging branch and broke it off. The branch unrolled into a scroll of paper in his hands. I couldn't see the paper clearly from my perch, but I saw writing on it, words.

"Oh, no," said Jack, his voice all tremolo. "It's everywhere. It should have burned away."

He spun around in circles and collapsed upon his knees. I grabbed the handle of the truck, but it broke off into a shard of paper. The paper had some writing on it, like a journal, dated, in the handwriting I recognized. "June 14th," it said. "This face is made of armor, but the leather isn't real. The animal that made the leather died an awful death. I can't help breaking everything I touch. I want to die but not be killed. I'm guessing it will be the latter. All I have to make myself is paper. All I have are words and my creations. Words are nothing in the face of liars, are they now? This face is made of armor, but the papyrus has died an awful death."

Then I looked up and Jack was spinning desperately around, his hands clutched over his eyes. The leaves were wafting down like coupling notes. The scene was blurry from the cab but still I recognized the gun. I saw Jack's hands and how they fumbled on its awful crutch. I screamed and pressed my face against the glass. The static of the radio began to sound like a crackling Christmas fire. The moose was being lifted from the road by wind, like just a piece of refuse. I tried to find a way out of the truck but everything I touched broke off, all scrawled with bits of Jack's old writings, like a will.

I screamed his name. "Please, Jack! Don't go!"

He spun around and put the gun into his mouth. I heard an awful pop. And then he was confetti. All the air around me was a wedding, just a nuptial white.

But then there was no Jack.

Photograph: Boys

Month four. My hands on Jack were like a potter's hands on clay. My hands were firing bricks then lining wells so I could drink before I parched. I grabbed him by the balls that could detach. I grabbed him by the neck that I could shepherd with my crook. Jack said: "A boy is as elusive as a superhero. I can't be seen unless I'm on a boxcar, tramping, when the wheels are moving and the world you know is spinning quickly by. I can't be seen unless I'm leaving town, unless I'm vilified in someone's longing, or I'm perfect in her memories obscured." I grabbed the placket of his shirt. It melted into vellum in his sweat. I worked his buttons open. I ran my hands over the wifebeater he always wore. I felt the muscles in his chest and birdcage of his ribs. I ran my palms over his chest. My mouth began to rock on him, a trombone slide. It shaped into the words I couldn't say — oh, stay, Jack, *stay.* My lips began to mutely chant and pray. "Don't tell me what this doesn't mean," I finally said. "Don't run us into ruin."

3. How Girls Find God

A girl was blowing out the Jesus candles on her cake. I don't know how I walked to where she was, but night had turned to day and I was picking bits of paper from my hair. The Jesus candles had burned down so that they looked decapitated.

"Isn't that a sacrilege?" I asked the girl, "To burn those Jesus candles on your cake?"

"And who are you? A dirty whore?" she asked. I counted up the candles. There were six of them. "I won the pinkest cake down at the cakewalk," said the girl. "I bet you never won a cake."

"Is it your birthday?" I asked, sweetly as I could. I hoped that she would give me cake.

"My birthday's right on Christmas," said the girl. "So I get Jesus candles on my cake. Why do you have that snow all over your hair?"

"For Christmas," I said. I was starving, and I wanted everything the girl could give me.

"Christmas doesn't come until next week," she said. "Do you like playing dolls?"

"I don't know how."

"I got to open up some presents early, and I got these dolls." She pointed to a space beside her on the ground. There must have been two dozen dolls. They all wore pink and were complete.

"How do you play?" I asked.

"You take their arms and legs and break them off," she said. "Before the boys come over and do it. Then you put the legs into the crawl space and you leave them there forever. Want to play? It's funner than a card game."

"But if you break them off, aren't *you* complicit in the crime?" I asked.

"What language are you speaking?" asked the girl.

ORIGAMI STRIPTEASE

She licked a line of frosting from her finger. "Are you one of those mealy Unitarians?"

"I want to play the game with you," I said.

And then the girl looked happy and a little mischievous. The girl dredged frosting on the bottom of a Jesus candle, and she stuck it in my mouth. She took a doll and beat it on a stump so that its head fell off. She held another by its hair and flung it to the sky, so that it fell and broke into a pile of parts.

"The pink kind tastes like cherries," said the girl, but it did not. It tasted like the white kind with a color added to it.

Minutes passed while we enjoyed the dolls and cake. I broke the legs off of the dolls like I was snapping string beans for a boiling pot. But then we had to go inside because the wind blew up a sudden paper rain. The rain had followed me through half the forest but had ceased when I had made it to the clearing near her house. I thought that it was gone, but here it was again. The girl made squeaky noises like she'd melt if she got wet, or inked, or spoiled. It was like after-nuclear white soot, the trail of Jack's undoing tracking me. I thought of how the next day—The Day After—is so relevant to scientists, when really the day after is a million days. A day that recreates into the next. The girl had noticed I had idiosyncratic snow coating my hair, but I could not convince her of the paper moose, although she listened to my tale like it was very tall.

"I might believe in crayons and wood," she said. "But paper is too silly now."

I watched as her diminutive soft hands took one leg and another leg and shoved them in the crawl space from the tiny door beside her room. She was efficient as an old conductor shoveling coal into an engine. The space was filled with legs that didn't crawl.

"I bet you want to fix the snow," she said. She grabbed her plastic brush and groomed my hair as bits of paper Jack fell out onto the floor. I grabbed the pieces and I stuffed them in my pocket. We had mangled all the dolls but no boys came. "They will," she said. "And if you want to fix the snow, there is a magic that can fix a broken thing. You don't know I do magic, but I do. I'll show you if you trust me. Do you?"

"Yes," I said. "You gave me so much cake."

"Then close your eyes and spin around and count to seven donkeys," said the girl.

She put a blindfold on my eyes and twirled me round. I must have fallen into momentary syncope then. When I awoke, I found myself surrounded by a hundred legs and splintered wooden beams. I looked behind me and there was an archway and a bed, my bed, though it was not my room the way I knew. The door back to the girl's room had a lock. I banged my fist against a rattling latch.

"This isn't funny, little brat!" I yelled.

It seemed that no one on the other side could hear. I heard the whispers and the music boxes playing Chopin on their goosebump rolls. I heard a gaggle of the giggling little girls, their stomping feet, the music boxes of perpetual insipid ballerinas. I heard her ripping paper from her latest presents. "Thank you, Bethany!" I heard her shout. And "Thank you, Kate! I always wanted a Mongolian tea tray!" She was so mannerly, exceedingly well-spoken with her guests. "Let's put our sleeping bags down now!" she said. "Let's play the séance game! Let's make somebody levitate!"

I knew what they were doing then. It was a game that all girls played, the way that boys played war. The girls were lighting candles and were circling one girl, probably the lightest one. The birthday girl would take the helm and put her fingers on the light girl's temples. "You are going to die tonight," she'd say. "Imagine how the car will hit your bicycle and you will fly away and die." The other girls would put two fingers from each hand beneath the light girl's body, cloaked in serious intent. "Now you are as light as feathers, stiff as boards," the birthday girl would say. And then they'd try to lift the girl with just their fingers. From my foxhole, I could barely hear their words but felt the sense of flying girls who thought they tasted cherry in the color pink. I pressed my ear against the door to see if I could hear.

"Let's pull off both her legs and give them to the boys," I heard her say. "There's nothing we can do to save her now. The car has hit her and she's dead in her imagination."

"Yes, yes!" the girls agreed. "Let's pull off both her legs."

The girls were ripping at the girl, I think, or maybe they were ripping me. I felt the ripping like it was my own.

And that's when I began to float away, my body boarded up and stiff as sleep.

Photograph: Girls

Month twenty-two.

It's not as if I thought a lot about it, grief. I used to think that we were one, the other girls and I. I didn't feel such jealousy about their perfect hair and sunshine smiles. But then I thought they were Jack's phantoms, keeping him away. Years back, he fucked this girl named Jennifer, and so I brought her home after he left. Her hair was bluish underneath the black. Her lips were rough and dry. I knew how easily her blood would flow to them, like speech, to steal into my mouth. "Do you like girlie-girls?" I asked. Her eyes were marbles shot out of their rings. She nodded, but her head was whip-stitched on. I slid my hand beneath her skirt. Oh, what a doll she was, immaculate. I grabbed a pair of scissors. I didn't care about the panties I was slicing off. They slithered down so I could see how shaved her pussy was. It felt as soft as lint from cotton clothes. She made these mewling kitten sounds. She said, "I'm drunk." I pulled away but she said, "No—demolish me." I started cutting up her skirt. I wanted to make it look like she'd been raped. I hated her, but then I wanted to be kind. I rubbed my fingers on her breasts. I slid my tongue beneath the smoothness of her pussy lips. I held her lumpy wrists. Possession was so easy, taking her and being her. She was like black ice on a bridge at night. I closed my eyes on her and, in slow motion, died.

4. How Boys Find God

The boys unloaded sacks of legs and paper snow that they had fingered from the girl's house. I saw their awful skirmish while I drifted from the house. One girl was scissoring the small girl's clothes away from her. The boys had ambushed them just as the girl was cutting off the pants into a pair of shorts so that the little minions would have access to the legs. They didn't mean to kill her but to whittle her, and yet, the girl was dead in her imagination. The other girls had moved unconsciously from plastic legs to real.

The boys had hatcheted the door that led to all the legs. They threw the music boxes down and cracked them with a bat. The girls were screaming and were swinging turkey knives. The boys wore pirate patches on their eyes and war paint on their cheeks. They grabbed the birthday girl before they left, and threw her in a burlap sack. They dragged her kicking, screaming with the legs to where the hideout was. The other girls were crying in the house, except the girl who thought that she was dead. That girl felt nothing of the incident and never would — unless she stepped into a tight unyielding hug that turned her body into tears.

The birthday girl did not take long to get her wits inside the bag.

The girl was wily, and she knew the magic that could make one's problems disappear. She worked her magic, and the legs became stealth bomber planes, the kind that look like sting rays. The sack was emptied in the cavern near the forest. The boys were not as angry as the girl had thought. The model planes were not as large as normal planes. The boys began to act like boys and spun the planes around and made annoying war sounds. Inside the cave, the darkness made it hard to etch out shapes, but she could see the boys careening further down the tunnel. She followed them through grappling darkness that held tiny dusty bits of light like shiny coal. Once in the brilliant light, the boys and girl saw that the legs were simply legs.

"You see?" The girl said to the boys. "Boys are hysterical and girls are not!"

She held the legs as proof. They were not war planes, not at all. But still, the legs resembled war more than the reckless game of urge the boys had played. And this is what they could not stand, this transformation of intent. Each boy was handling nothing but a piece of plastic girl. Each one felt tricked, as if he was responsible for breakage he did not intend. The boys had only tried to play a game.

"'We're not the way you think," the boys retorted, rolling up their sleeves.

She gave them magic stares out of her stark, hypnotic eyes. And then, the boys began to evidence hysteria. They held their hands to foreheads and they fainted, or just hopped around and screamed and spoke of stomach pain. They limped and cackled and showed classic signs of neurasthenia. They sunk onto the ground and promptly passed into a place of rock, which led them to the Art Room. An origami truck was rolling down the hill and scared the girl, because it seemed to be unmanned. She ran off screaming toward her house. The boys walked sullenly into the Art Room.

"It's piñata time," the supervisor said, and handed them balloons. The lights were flickering the way they do in subway cars.

The Art Room might have been an old familiar place, but it was not exactly that. The boys, however, seemed to know that there were weigh stations filled up with boys, lost boys who needed art. The first thing the boys noticed was the lack of breath. To blow balloons one had to use a helium machine. The supervisor blew a huge balloon to make the body of the ox. The smaller ones were for the

ORIGAMI STRIPTEASE

ox piñata's legs. The Art Room was the place where Jack had been since he had shot himself. He clutched his bag of scraps, the paper with his writing on it.

"Now Jack," the supervisor said. "It's time to let us touch your paper scraps."

Jack held the bag protectively. The Art Room had a rule that all one's things became communal. The boys stirred glue of flour and water to stick paper from Jack's bag onto balloons to make the ox. They laid their colorful crepe paper on his words. He crawled inside the paper ox, that Trojan Horse—the gift that persecutes the one who takes it in. Jack knew the way to curl into a shell beneath a hundred brutal fists. They hung the ox piñata from the center rafter.

"Let's beat it to a pulp," the supervisor said.

So Jack began to feel the battering of sticks. The boys were doing what they knew to do. They swung their sticks and killed the color from the thing that they had made.

Photograph: Glass Bowl

The white doves talked about my body like it was a piece of flint. They rubbed my disembodied legs and checked their dripping bags. I was a cheap and flattened penny they picked off the railroad tracks. They darted in and out of sound waves, so I thought of dragon-flies. I thought of how I could be skimming over water in a luminescent hovercraft of my own flesh. The days were long the way that reeling in a fish is long. There was a pinched white smell all over me. It was the stuff around gefilte fish, a Yiddish name of something cloudy, sneezed against the palate of the day. I knew that I was something in a jar, both far away and near. *If you won't kill me,* I thought, hoping thoughts would make a monitor respond, *just kill the awful fishbowl glass.* I heard the chugging cylinders and beeps. There was a pretty bow that tied itself around each day, infinity.

5.

"I am a small recycled microcosm trying to save my life," a voice said out of nowhere.

I heard my body falling like a broken kite. It made a tiny flapping sound, the sound of paper being buffeted. I was both featherweight and board. There were a million bits of paper floating by me like a blizzard. Once I hit the ground I started rolling, like the ground was hilly, but it looked to me like it was flat. Each time I tried to stand I lurched into a snowy absence, flailing, with my arms like windshield-wiper blades. When I found solid footing and the snow cleared long enough for me to have a view, I saw that Jack was pushing on a curvy piece of glass and running like a gerbil. I was so happy to see him alive, I stumbled toward him but kept falling on the way.

"Oh, Jack!" I screamed. "I thought that you were dead!" Each time his legs sped up, I rolled a little closer to his feet. "Is this a gerbil ball?" I asked. "How did you come alive again?"

But Jack did not respond. He ran in rote attention to his task. "A piece of me remained," said Jack. "And now I am a small recycled microcosm trying to save my life."

The shredded paper shook around us like a blizzard and a little plastic house was tumbling by our side. A plastic tree kept landing on my back and poking me. My legs got tangled in the little plastic fence.

"What do you mean?" I asked. "Is this sphere yours? Is this one yours?"

"It's coming," Jack said ominously. "Help me run." I didn't see the threat at all, but ran beside him at a hurried pace.

"What's coming, Jack?" I asked. "Please, talk to me."

"The hand," said Jack. "The hand's more personal than switch or staff."

"What hand?"

"The hand is vengeful but the hand is kind. How can we reconcile with the hand?"

"Who is the hand?" I asked. The scenery whizzed by us as we ran. We rolled down hills and over streets. "The hand the hand the *hand*," said Jack, as if the hand were something I should know.

We rolled onto a movie set. The walls were black and white. "Oh, no," said Jack. And then I felt the lifting of the hand.

Jack tried to run but none of his quick motions moved us forward. The giant fingers clasped around the globe that we were in. The monstrous eye peered in at us like we were captive in a zoo.

"We're in the movie," Jack said. "It's the allegory about memory and loss." The hand was cocking back, then flinging us against a broken space. "Oh, God," said Jack. "We're turning into movie stills in dreams."

And then we fell into the crash. The glass had shattered everywhere. The paper snow inside the globe was falling with its bits of Jack's own words. The tree and house and fence were falling down. And just as I glanced back, I saw the audience and theater and popcorn lifting toward the open mouths. I saw them watching us upon the screen.

I heard the voice inside the screen. "Rosebud," it said. One enigmatic word.

Photograph: Up

"Let's lift her up," I heard them say.

Was it the séance game? I felt the sound of something cracking on my head, as if a mallet banged
a gong to wake the monks from hollow limbs of
monasteries. The doves were shaking me. *Wake
up,* I thought. Within the synesthesia of the accident inside my brain, I heard a bell and saw the
color red. I thought perhaps that I was rising up,
diaphanous, a photograph that's suddenly
exposed to light before it hits the fixative. This
photograph—was it the girl who died before the
wily animals dragged her away? *I saw that girl,* I
tried to scream, to tell the doves. *I know her name.
She's worthy: lift her up.*

6. What Made Jack Run

Jack pulled the petals back.

"It tastes like cherries," Jack said to the bud.

I'm guessing that his tongue was only tasting white. The room was clear as water, full of minerals settled long ago. He slid his tongue between the papery bits of red. He spread them open wide.

"Rosebud," said Jack. One enigmatic word.

"How did you get into my room?" I asked.

But I had heard him coming, and I'd gotten ready to play hide without the seek. When I had seen his truck outside and heard his footsteps on the stairs, I'd scooped up all the legs and thrown them out the window. I crawled around and checked beneath the bed. I checked the closets and the gaps behind the radiators. I watched them twist and twirl in air.

"Be gone, girl legs," I said.

I shut the blinds and prayed that he would never know about the awful broken legs I'd kept. They lodged like sickle cells inside the tunnels of my flesh—the haunted, fractured, foreign parts of me I could not exorcise. No matter where I went, the legs had found their way to me like migratory crabs that follow sidewalks to the ocean.

"What did yours say?" I asked him cautiously. "Did she give good advice?"

"She said that I should tell you all the secret things I think about," said Jack. "She said that I am ready. And I am."

"Then did you bring your writing here?" I asked. We used the talking tricks that we had learned.

"I did," said Jack. "But let's go tit for tat. What did yours say?"

Mine had a shuttered office with a simple chair and couch, and I could lie to her by speaking jargon. I had twisted her around a sentence, easily.

"She said that I was ready too," I said.

I liked how we'd begun to use these words: "connected," "intimacy," "dialogue," and "issues." It made me feel like we were speaking the same tongue, and not a speech of misbegotten petals. Jack seized my hand and pressed it in his hands. He grabbed the stack of writings.

"It's all in here," said Jack. "I'll let you see. I *want* it. To be close."

He'd taken pains to glue the pieces right. He'd gathered them from all around the shredded place. He'd taped and organized and glued them to cohesion. I registered the gravity of what we were about to do. And then I took his words and finally read. I read Jack's words that spoke of love and want and loss. I read about his awful fears. I read—quite simply—Jack. His words were plain and eloquent and honest. They told about the brutal ways that he'd been hurt. They told about the tiny ways that he had hoped. I read them to the final line. I looked at him, his plaintive stare. As open as he seemed, I still believed he must be holding something back, the way I hid the legs.

"She loves me," Jack said, pulling out a petal from beneath the thorny wait. "Or does she love me not?"

He took his hand and guided mine to where his tongue had been. He showed me what was soft, and wet, and gentle as a guided start. He took my hand into his hand. I felt alive and fully there. We leaned into a kiss.

But then there was an awful crash, cacophony of glass.

That's when the legs came back, the boomerangs of legs. The legs came flying through the window like a slew of vampire bats. They battered us, and slapped our ears, and cut our hands apart. Jack ducked and dodged around the room. I sat as mute as toast. And that's when Jack had grabbed his words and ran. I watched him run until the evening folded up into a paper bow. Until the distance was accordioned. Until the whole world folded up into an origami fan, and put out all the gentle heat of hands with plastic hands.

Part 4:
How to Play Hangman
with the Moon

1.

The light came flooding into me. I felt the sickles fleeing from my veins. A television perched above me like an elder owl. The walls were scrubbed with supernatural sheen. The fragile, sterile garments bustled in the hall — expedient with coolers full of blood. "Where'd Jack go?" I asked quickly when a thin-lipped nurse strode in. "What are you doing with my sheets?" She jumped back from the shock of my coherent voice, then started chattering as if awakenings were nothing more than blips upon her daily screen. I'd washed up on the shoreline of my life again.

"Oh sweetheart, Jack left days ago. He caught an early flight to see the ice cap in Kangerlussuaq. All week, he sat beside you in this chair and told you stories about dogsledding in Thule and sleeping in the igloo village. Some of us would crowd around and listen on our breaks. Can you imagine? Greenland! None of us will ever get to go." The nurse took vital signs. "He also said to tell you — *when* you came out of the coma — that his transplant was successful. He is going to see the ice hotel." I had an image of an icy version of *The Graduate* in which I rode my own Iditarod to reach a distant ice hotel and found Jack in a chapel made of ice, his tongue stuck to a frozen bride as if she were a metal pole. I grabbed at hanging icicles and shook the chapel into cubes and screamed his name and picked her off of him. Jack's tongue was tipped with frostbite as he started frenching me.

The nurse said, "Dear, your legs are here, beneath the sheet. You feel them, darling? Here?" She kneaded them like she was rolling cookie dough.

"What transplant? Yes, I feel my legs. They're waterlogged."

"Jack got a donor heart," the nurse chirped giddily,

171

as if she'd known us both for years. She rubbed my kneecaps and my calves. "The gloaming is a heavy place," she said. "And it will drain from you." She sprung up toward the door. I heard her voice exclaiming, "Look, she burst out talking! Doctor!" Then three doctors hurried in. Their stethoscopes were ready. "Now breathe in," they said in unison. "Breathe out."

They asked me who would pick me up, and I pretended I would call a friend, then dialed a cab. I signed the discharge papers, then I waited by the smoking orderlies outside. The cab drove through the old downtown, which had been razed and filled with trees and grass. Then finally, we pulled up to my house. I yanked off the police tape, and I jammed the key into the lock. I thought the house would be in shambles, overturned and fingerprinted, but it wasn't. It was simply stripped. The Sludge had only left enough to quell suspicion from the cops when they arrived. My table stood defiantly alone, and on it was the cast-iron pan. *A coma, if it doesn't kill you, heals whatever's wrong.* That's what the doctor said to me when I woke up. I was not healed. I still felt dizzy and unwell. My kidneys were two cardboard chairs, my heart a paper valentine. I had to lean against the table just to keep from falling on the floor, and then I longed for my old furniture to prop me up. I lay down on the floor beside the table leg and stared up at the ceiling for a while. I thought about Jack's heart. So much had changed. If they replaced Jack's heart, did any love for me remain? It was a goofy thought, borne out of insecurity, but still I wondered. How would Jack react if I spoke plainly, simply said, "I love you, Jack. I love you more than I have ever loved?" The thought of saying it, quite frankly, made me want to puke. Why can't we just speak plainly, from the heart? Why is the goal to always bypass?

I thought the house would be more dusty or forbid-

ORIGAMI STRIPTEASE

ding, but it wasn't that. I walked into the kitchen and my body started shaking as I thought about the night two weeks ago. I'd reconstructed some of it from things the doctors told me, but the last few moments were a rush of light and sound. I did remember thinking that I'd lived and Speck had died. Speck was the one who brought me to the hospital that night he almost killed me. The doctor told me how he carried me and told them I was very frail. My head bled the way a bag of garbage breaks, and blood was everywhere — my blood — throughout the car, still clinging to the walls. I wondered if I'd ever have the energy to clean it off. Then Speck had left me in the hospital. As soon as I was speak-ing, cops began to question me. They said — based on the little evidence — "it could be hard to prosecute your *girl*friend." Speck had the chance to wipe things down. They did not have a single record of "domestic" calls from my address, and Speck had taken care of me. The wound — as Speck had claimed — was quite consistent with a falling pot rack from a shaky beam.

They had my bloody garb inside a plastic bag, and gave that to me when I left. They also had my wallet and my keys.

"Another thing," the doctor said. "Jack wanted you to take his specimen."

He led me to a walk-in cooler in the hospital. Inside, there were a bunch of labeled plastic bags. "Mostly from amputees," the doctor said. He handed me a jar and inside was a heart. "So there it is. Enjoy your bloody Valentine."

When I got home, I set the heart beside the cast-iron pan. They'd put it in a Mason jar, like fresh preserves.

Speck only left one thing I cared about: The Naked Pen. I guessed that he felt guilty, knowing that he almost did me in. In truth, I didn't really want her and her ani-mated ways. The pen seemed like a soppy drunken housewife who could not be bothered to be fully clothed.

She languished near a blotter, starved for ink. She watched me do my slow ablutions to the gods of sickness. She seemed so old and broken now, a woman with one purpose that was rote and tired and not, and never, spiritual. The pen had not eked out a piece of thoughtful prose in quite some time. Having her around would make me think about the different grades of nakedness. Anyone can strip a pen, or write the wooden language of a midnight fuck.

Despite debility, I did a lot of things those next two weeks. I plugged into the gossip mill to find news on Jack. I had a carpenter come in to put up shelves. I only had one curio besides the pen—Jack's heart—but wanted to display it properly. The carpenter devised a case in which I placed a little freezer with a see-through door, then put the heart inside. I also went to Hornet's, and I got some oddities to put around my house: an ostrich-feather hat, a well-dinged copper bowl, and one carved wooden spoon. I even fucked one boy who'd wandered from the borderlands. They called him Marsh and he was not a talker, but he'd heard of me. "The woman left for dead," he said. "The phantom literatus brought to life."

Between these bursts of energy, I rested constantly. Each gesture made me feel as if I stepped into a chamber drained of oxygen. The Sludge had left the bed in which I'd sucked his cock, the room in which he'd beaten me. The bedroom was too full of anguish, and I only went in there to sleep, but not to rest. I rested on the hardwood floor, a pillow propping up my head. I couldn't seem to wash the smell of hospital away, but maybe it was better than the other smells. The nutmeg of The Sludge's kindness in the kitchen. The cumin of his rage.

And then Jack's letter came. "I'll be there in twelve days," it read. "To figure out the koan: does love come free? Does Freelove know? I want to see you; meet me. Jack."

ORIGAMI STRIPTEASE

How could I figure out that riddle?

I knew that I'd concocted fantasies to think that love was all it promised. Was this wrong? Or was it similar to how queer people mapped out organs from chimerical desires? I feared that Jack and I would be too different to talk. I had his troubled heart, I had my crumbling body, and I kept both in my hollowed house. He'd seen inside my broken skull. So what if Jack was healed, and I was still so fractured? But he'd come though, hadn't he? How did he know to come? And what about the rumor I had heard, about his artsy girlfriend and her stylish shoes?

2.

I acted like the organ meant something to me, because I had to think such things. I had to think that Jack had given it to me the way a fairground lover gives half of a metal heart. At night, I held the jar against my chest and tried to feel what it contained. I held it like a conch shell to my ear but then I set it down, afraid my fingers were too slippery and it would shatter into EKG waves on the floor. If I had listened to the heart I might have noticed that it told a story, but I didn't know the way to listen to a heart and its iambic voice, especially a heart entombed and separate from Jack. The heart contained the story of the pathogenesis. It went like this:

The ice storm had turned all the streets to melamine. The trees slid out from hugs. The houses were dumped out of a Monopoly game, so uniform that children dreamed of opening the wrong door and forgetting which home was their own, then being severed from their parents and swept off to foster care. No one could walk down sidewalks without courting tailbone injuries. It was the seventies and Jack was ten. The husbands traded in their shovels for guitars, and streets were not plowed for the weekend as the faithful had relinquished organized religion. Children pulled their siblings on small sleds. The kids all loved the ice storm. They lived for the divinations of a weather-vengeful God. There were some tragedies each winter, though. A populist law was enacted for the kids under the age of twelve, as frankly, parents thought the governance of trees was adequate. The cold made the guardians too reckless. "Just have fun!" they told the kids, as they prepared to toke it up with seven long-haired neighbors who would singe the carpet shag then laugh about it later. "Button up your coats."

It might be easy, looking back, to criticize the level of

ORIGAMI STRIPTEASE

distraction, but the kids loved being sent into the grim Grimm landscape, even if they should have been afraid.

Then again, there were some casualties.

The year before, the search and rescue crew had found a boy encased in ice. The kid looked like a prank fly in a plastic ice cube, as if he had been put there as a tasteless joke. He had been missing for a week. The kids—had they been searching—would have checked the lake, but parents were naïve. They prayed and cried and thought of Santa Claus and hollow Christmases with lumps of coal replacing children's laughter in the house. In other words, they panicked and thought only of themselves. Their instincts for the thought processes of a child were gone, an absence that they grieved in flagellating self-absorption. Meanwhile, the kid had fallen through the ice and drowned. He floated face first up against the coating on the lake. And since the freezing season had just started taking hostages, another layer froze around the boy and trapped him there. He grimaced in that picture frame of ice, an image deemed too "shocking" for the local paper at the time. The negatives were put into a vault at the *Gazette.* It was a very merry Christmas for the children, who were happy every time it was somebody else's kid.

But Jack was not so happy when the ice storm came. His throat was raw with strep and nobody would take him to the doctor. His parents were too busy getting high.

"Most people get a tickle in the throat when it's so cold," his mother said.

Jack wondered what it was about adults, why they called every atom bomb a tickle. Sure, it's a cliché, and sure, it happens all the time, but it is not that simple when the tickle is invading you, your flesh and private self. His parents liked to tickle Jack in places that no cold war had discovered yet. He lived in terror of their hands. Their hands were bombs dressed up as friendly fire. The tunnels of Jack's body knew the wire brush of the evil chimney sweeps, and he had felt the creosote of everyone's denial in the interim. Jack had the body of a choirboy, an angelic face and lips that always looked ashamed. Abusers must choose children who are flushed and shy, who have the look of guilt when they have never done a thing but pray to faggot Jesus for relief. Most times, the tickling happened at his parents' parties. The invitation list included a sadistic Egyptologist, one defrocked priest who had been shunned by his parishioners, Jack's parents, the farm auctioneer who later died of emphysema, Doctor Tackus the podiatrist, Jack's brother Rob, and three professors who were doing military-funded research at the local bison farm. They ushered Jack into a topsy-turvy world, the kind of place where a baptismal is a frozen lake and dying as a photograph inside a court's manila envelope gave notoriety to children who were never thought about again. It shouldn't be politely said, but Jack was raped. Yes, Jack was raped by them. His heart knew this.

The ice had lingered on for seven days.

Jack couldn't really talk. His throat was narrowing with strep. He felt it like a broken telescope, the kind of pain that only stargazers can understand. His mom had given him a pad of paper and a pen. "Can I go see the doctor?" Jack wrote on the pad. His mother took his temperature.

"Jack, honey, you're not boiling over yet," she said. "Let's wait a few more hours." Jack wanted to be in the hospital.

He knew there was a party planned that night. His father hated having any of his parties interrupted. The partygoers joked that Jack was really "straight" if he refused the drugs. Jack knew that some of them would trip that night and maybe do their rituals. He wanted to be far away from them, with some maternal nurse. It was a perfect night for dropping LSD. Some people in the

ORIGAMI STRIPTEASE

neighborhood had strung up Christmas lights before the ice storm and most lights were trapped inside the ice, so that they cast an eerie convalescent glow. Each year, there was a competition over Christmas lights, and all the cynics wished bad fortune on the winners of the contest. One house caught fire from overloaded wires, and this made every bitter Scrooge heart feel self-righteous.

"Fuck the paradigm of darkness and the light," the Egyptologist exclaimed while passing Rob the pipe. "Where is your little skull-and-crossbones lighter? Light a buzz for Rob, Jack-Lynn." Jack did as he was told and flicked the flame out of his thumb so Rob could get a burn. "You are an angel made of ash, Jack-Lynn," the Egyptologist exclaimed. "Come sit on Uncle Pharaoh's lap."

"Not now," scrawled Jack, and held the pad of paper up.

"Well aren't we uppity when we have got the written word!" laughed Uncle Pharaoh, pulling Jack's reluctant body toward his own. "Come on, sit down, you little shit."

Jack knew it always started with a similar cliché. The wire brush, then the creosote, then pushing, scraping wire. The endless sweeping out around the burn. They all pretended that the world was made of humble chimney sweeps, but it was made of lecherous adults. His throat hurt so much then: he feared someone might puncture it by making him suck cock. He hated that he could not scream, not that he ever did, but it was different knowing that the option wasn't there. He climbed onto The Pharaoh's lap. The man held Jack's butt tight against his bulge, so Jack would know. He'd know that coming never came without comeuppance.

Rob stared out at the moon. He wore a dopey grin. He acted like he didn't know the bloated moon was just as sinister as salmon roe on some rich person's plate. The full moon spawned unbridled violence that went on

179

right beneath its watchful eye. The cosmos didn't care if The Pharaoh held Jack tight against a wall and forced things into him.

That was the photograph Jack always carried in his mind, the boy and moon. Jack hoped that everyone would get so wasted they would be too out of it to do satanic things to him. He sunk down in his skin and prayed to the indifferent moon. It was a strangulating skein of light. He wanted to cry. Rob stood up and he blew a film onto the window glass and started sketching caricatures of people from the party on the backdrop of the moon. Rob drew a different profile in each pane of four, like Andy Warhol's Marilyns. The Pharaoh had a dick hard as a rolling pin, a secret household weapon that made dough out of Jack's legs. Jack cringed in fear. He had no weapon of his own. Adults were sprawled out on the floor. They looked like they were making a mass grave. Jack wished they were all dead, and he pretended that they were. It was a thought he thought about some years after that night. He hated them.

Then Uncle Pharaoh said to Rob, "Have you played hangman with the moon?" A piece of ash was floating lazily from The Pharaoh's pipe. The Pharaoh smashed it in his fist, which made Jack think of highway flares, and of the wreckage he was in.

"What's that?" asked Rob.

Rob was amazing. He had rock-star hair. He was as pretty as a calendar. The men all loved to take him into the basement, to the mattress in the paneled room. Jack's parents passed a tiny firefly flame between their lips, the kind of flame you want to smear against a wall, a flame that isn't anything but insect ass and guts. A roach. An awful pathogenic vector of a burn.

"We hang you in a tree and jerk you off," The Pharaoh said. "You'll get more high than you have ever been." He opened up his palm, and there was nothing there. The little highway flare was gone.

ORIGAMI STRIPTEASE

Rob looked suspicious for a moment. "Lynch somebody else," he finally said and shook his head disgustedly.

"We can't hang *her*," The Pharaoh said. His eyes became hypnotic spinning plates. "She's got nothing to jerk. Come on, I want to get you high like that. Just trust me. It's incomparable."

He knew Rob would capitulate. Jack marveled at the fact that Rob seemed like he didn't mind when partygoers made him suck their dicks or touch their wives. Rob really liked it when he got to play with Jack, *Jack-Lynn* his *sister,* and could tumble foreign girl parts in his hands. "Okay, man, sure," said Rob. "Just let me smoke again."

"I'm not going along," Jack wrote, and held the paper up for The Pharaoh.

"Oh?" The Pharaoh asked, then took the lighter, lit the corner of Jack's note, and tossed it in the ashtray. "Your opinion burns."

"Cool," said Rob, and slapped The Pharaoh five. "Looks like you got the shortest straw," he said to Jack, and glanced between Jack's legs. "Or should I say, the nonexistent straw." They laughed. Jack gave a little wave to Mom and Dad. Neither of Jack's parents understood infectious muteness.

The tree was standing by the lake, a venerable maple. Jack thought it looked as lonely as a TV Indian. The Pharaoh put the coil of rope over his arm. The rope already had a noose on it. Back then, all people played with rope, but mostly to make hangers for their plants. Rob brought the folding chair. When they drove stoned, Jack fantasized about his death. He thought the crash would happen in a cloud of smoke, and he would simply turn to dust. He wanted to be dead right then. His brother was fourteen but sometimes drove. Rob stuffed his pants with potholders, the kind that Girl Scouts made.

Jack knew his brother loved to masturbate because the walls were thin. It made Jack happy when he heard the sounds. He thought that even if he left the world by cutting up his arms with razor blades, his brother would survive and maybe just forget he ever had a sister. Jack-Lynn was an illusion. There was no sister anyway, just ashen face and ash-singed name.

Rob climbed up on the chair, and The Pharaoh put the noose around his neck.

Jack thought that Rob had always been the fearless one. Rob made pretend dead-person faces, acting like his neck was broken, lolling to the side. This cracked The Pharaoh up since he was high. Jack wished that he were high. He hadn't brought his pad of paper so he couldn't ask The Pharaoh for a smoke. The build-up was intolerable. He squeezed his hand together in his pocket as he waited for his role. Then quietly, The Pharaoh grabbed his arm and led him to the tree.

"As soon as I say pull, you pull," he said.

He took Jack's brother's trousers and his boxers to his knees, then yanked the chair away and shouted, "pull." Jack knew exactly how to work his dick. It didn't take a lot of skill—a circus monkey could have done the job. Jack couldn't look up at Rob's gagging, bloated face. He simply worked the tool. He watched their wispy breath get tangled in the cold.

"Go on now, Yank," The Pharaoh said in an affected British accent. "Yank."

Jack wasn't sure what moment things turned as they did, but suddenly, Rob's body wasn't tensing anymore. "Pharaoh, let him down," Jack crackled from his throat, and took his hand off of Rob's dick.

The lake seemed oddly quiet without the summer insects and the frogs. Jack never went there in the wintertime. He saw smoke signals coming from uncertain chimney stacks. Smoke gathered in the sky before the

182

hieroglyphs made sense, and then they looked just like the remnants of an old train, taking prisoners away. After Jack made his statement, he walked slowly toward the lake, and thought he might walk right across until he found a weak spot in the ice. He heard The Pharaoh howling in the background, "God, what have we done, Jack-Lynn? I think we broke his neck. Don't leave me here."

He heard the thudding of the two joined bodies on the ground. He hoped the knife The Pharaoh used to cut his brother down went through The Pharaoh's heart. He could have felt a lot of things but then, he mostly just felt righteous. *Yeah,* he thought, *I told you bastards so.*

Jack tested out a corner of the ice. He thought he'd walk on water, prove himself a miracle, or else he'd die and be a martyr; it was all a coin toss anyway. He turned around to glimpse The Pharaoh clutching Rob and wailing, hitting things with fists and panicking. *That's right,* he thought. *Freak out, you murderer, you rapist.* Jack stepped carefully on ice-skate lines, the cursive elegy of someone's happy childhood. He felt calm when he thought how they'd find him in the lake, faceup but peaceful, like a smiling saint. The ice was probably too thick and he was probably too light, but he could try to court the other side. Each tragedy had happened anyway. Each day was a cold day in hell.

"What do you think you're doing? Come back here, Jack-Lynn," he heard The Pharaoh yell. "You killed your brother. You can't run."

Jack turned around when he was midway out. He'd made a bull's-eye. *Kill me, too,* he thought. *I'll make it easy on your lazy eye.* His throat was still too weak to push out words. The center of the lake felt like a coliseum, and he wished somebody would release the lions. He wished the trees would cheer *ding dong the freak is dead* as he was ripped apart by feral claws. The Pharaoh paced along the bank then sat down on a picnic table that was capped with ice and snow. Jack thought about The Pharaoh's hard-on freezing off, and then his buzz unraveling. The Pharaoh was too glum to fight.

"Come on," he pleaded, stretching out his hand. "I know that you're upset, but we don't need a dead girl and a dead boy now. Two boys, I mean."

Jack felt a sense of satisfaction knowing that The Pharaoh was negotiating now, by calling him a boy, thus calling out his own, repellent faggotry. *That's right, you fucking moron,* he thought. *You rape boys.* The Pharaoh was so used to Jack's compliance and his silence that he didn't realize Jack couldn't shout back to the bank.

The Pharaoh was a coward. If Jack lay flat on his back and closed his eyes, The Pharaoh would split town and leave Jack with the evidence. Jack didn't care. A case of fratricide would keep the county riveted for months, perhaps distract the predators and lock him safe in juvenile detention for a while. The party was too high to know The Pharaoh had gone off with them. So Jack just spread his body on the ice, supine against the frozen shelf, and stared up at the constellations. He loved the stars but not enough to care about their names. He knew the dippers and Orion's belt, but that was it. He knew a lot of empty spaces and he knew a lot of belts, but none of them could stir the feeling of just staring at the sky. Jack wasn't sorry Rob was dead. His parents would pretend that they were sad. His mother would act devastated, but she wouldn't be that sorry over Rob, just sorry that she felt alone, that belts of stars held nothing of the absence in. They all were sorry for the same damn reason, loneliness. It wasn't selfless and it wasn't due to love.

The people were all frozen in their own still lakes. They were just awful photographs that turned the viewer's eyes to liquid, made him blind. Too shocking for the public eye.

"Jack-Lynn, I'm coming out. Stay put," The Pharaoh

said. "I'm going to rescue you. Come on, I love you, and your parents love you. We don't want you dead." He almost sounded kind.

Jack registered those words and felt the ice displace when The Pharaoh stepped out from the bank. He thought he felt the sooty water ripple underneath his back. He heard The Pharaoh breathing hard. The cold gave the illusion of thin air although they were not at an altitude. The Pharaoh wasn't huge, but he was paunchy. Gradually, The Pharaoh inched within five feet of Jack and poked him with a stick.

"Get up, Jack-Lynn, let's go," he said. "Jack-Lynn, this isn't funny. We'll be killed if we don't get our story straight. We have to have each other's backs. You've got to know the gravity of what you did."

Jack thought it would be funny if he was a mummy and The Pharaoh stood there poking him. He lay completely still and didn't open up his mouth. The Pharaoh spit out coils of breath.

"You're just in shock," The Pharaoh said. "We'll get you back to shore and take you home and fill you up with cocoa. Come on, I know you're sick, Jack, and this weather isn't good for you."

He'd never acted so parental, and he never called Jack "Jack." Jack liked the way it felt.

And then he heard the crack.

It sounded like a rifle underneath the ice, like it came from the belly of the lake and then shot out. Jack sat up quickly, but he was too late. He saw The Pharaoh plunge into the brackish blue. He tried to find The Pharaoh's stick, but he could not. The Pharaoh's eyes were desperate, pleading now. He held the lip of ice for just a moment, then it broke. "Say something! Call for help!" The Pharaoh sputtered as the water sucked him down. His arms were floundering for Jack but Jack stepped back.

"I can't," Jack rasped, and turned around.

PEGGY MUNSON

Though what he said was literal, it sounded negligent. He really could not shout for anyone. At first, Jack skidded toward the shore, as if to seek out help. But then the thought occurred to him that he could just escape. He ran until he lost his breath, but where would he have gone? He was a gerbil in a wheel. He trudged back home.

When the rheumatic fever came, two weeks after that day, the doctors said his heart and nervous system might have been affected or might show damage later. "You say that she was resting this whole time? You're sure?" the doctor asked his mother, telling her how strep could turn into rheumatic fever. The doctor tapped his pen against the chart. Jack felt the pressure rising up, like death, inside that one mercurial moment.

"Yes," she said. "But then, Jack-Lynn has had enormous stress these past two weeks."

"Of course," the doctor said.

His eyes teared up a little bit. The doctor knew. The whole town knew. They knew the Egyptologist had run off with Jack's brother and had murdered him, then thrown himself into the icy lake.

"We'll do whatever we can do," the doctor said.

Then nobody did anything.

3.

I still felt skittish in the house The Sludge had left, despite the fact that I was working on obtaining a restraining order. Who can decree restraint?

A battered women's group had come around and helped me with the papers and the lawyer's fees. A lot of the community had taken interest in my coma. The people of the borderlands adored a nouveau margin-dweller. Overnight I had become their token charity. My old tricks even had a benefit and bought me an electric scooter so I could have more mobility. But no one came around except for Mona Fingerhut, the magpie from the battered women's place, and all I thought from listening to her rant was that I must have turned into an animal. She drove me nuts with her empowerment rants. When Mona blathered on, I wanted to bite her on the neck because her rabid chatter made me think about The Sludge. I wanted to chomp, and growl, and howl, but I was sick of stories and of words. I wished that I could speak Coyote after all.

I also had an urge to chomp a hunk out of the meaty heart that Jack had left. I hated anything that called itself a muscle. Bad enough as nouns, when muscles turned to verbs they made a pulp of any simple aspiration coming from a quiet place of slack. The Sludge had muscled me until I almost died. The house itself felt atrophied, and flesh was draped on me like cloth. No one was humble, not the bricklayers of bones and not the tailors of my flesh. They all believed that they were helping me, because they gossiped and drew sketches of anatomy and poked and prodded me. But frankly, I was never more alone. I held the jar of heart and wished it were that easy to cut out, and cordon off, the damage that was done to me.

The next twelve days decreed restraint. I had to keep

from opening the jar of heart. I had to keep from taking out a screwdriver and disassembling what the boys had gotten me, the scooter that reminded me how sick I was. I had to keep from calling up The Sludge and telling him that I was ready now, was ready to be finished off. I know I should have been enthusiastic to have courted death and lived, but I was having trouble mustering a bit of gratitude. Reality was harder than the netherworld of where I'd been. I was a cripple: Speck was right. So how could I face Jack when he had been restored?

I only had a teeny light of hope.

There was a Tomb of the Unknown between my legs and there, there was a tiny flame I could not snuff. My body had been sanded to its undercoat, and underneath the bumps and holes was something more sublime: a thumping beat. Instead of reaching for a cock, I rubbed the Mason jar as if I had a genie bottle. When I did this, poppy fields appeared between my legs. I set the jar beside my bed and rubbed my pussy raw with want. I wanted Jack to fuck me with his new, and perfect, heart. Until I saw him, though, I fucked myself. I slid my fingers in. I hated how I could not fully reach inside myself. The angle wasn't right. My fist would not quite fit. I hated that I could not pull The Sludge's inky and distorted me outside of me. I hated that I did not have the exorcising hand.

4.

Each night, for twelve days straight, I dreamed of Jack.

I tried to climb to him, but I kept slipping on the ice. My hands had lost their palmistry. My shoes had shed their treads. The earth was mercilessly slick, and I kept thudding on my ass. I ran like someone in a water-barrel race. The chapel taunted me beyond a snowy field atop an ice-capped hill. My grandma's wedding dress got snagged on sharpened bits of ice and shredded: I looked like a pipeline whore. I tried to get some traction in the cold. *You have to sand it, give it tooth,* I thought: a tip from some home-renovation show. I had been fashioned from lagoons of orphaned driftwood, screwed together after being battered by a gang of waves. I was too many broken bits to go ahead. I was not worthy of free love without a heavy bill of lading: punishment of sharks and planks. I had to climb to him. The snow was falling all around and cloaking me. I had to get to Jack.

No handholds held. The ice was epidemic. It was mean and torturous and sliddery. One time, I made it ten feet forward then I slipped a good fifteen behind, as if I'd turned into a metal sphere sled or a seal. The Ice Chapel was glistening like a huge zirconium. The nurse had said that's where he'd gone. Between the chapel and my body was a field of ice and snow that rose and fell where wind had sculpted it. The wind was like a high-pitched whistle that burned out my eardrums even when inaudible to me. The spires of ice were breathtaking, but what I really loved was the stained "glass": the paneled ice that had been pigment-dyed. Each time I tried to climb—with antique lace and heels, not crampons—I slid further back. The ice did its banana-peel gag and my coccyx hit the ground. I had to meet Jack in a place he knew, not wait for all of it to thaw. I had to meet him while I slept, not wake again to hardwood floors and cast-iron pans.

PEGGY MUNSON

Not meet him in an angry world where I'd been sanded down to just my tooth, where any new adhesion took. I could not meet him in my own cryonic hell. I had to scale whatever ice was in the way to get to Jack.

I lifted up my skirt and tried to run. But then, my feet took air. I heard my body land. The ice slid down my thigh and chilled me to the core. I slipped away, slid belly-first and backward down the grade. "Jaaaaack," I screamed.

I woke up bathed in sweat. The glacial world had melted into me, and I was drenched. But finally, twelve days were up.

5.

The gnats were gathering in lassoed heat, then scattering. I knew that if I stared too long at headstones, they would start to look like torsos, and I feared my heavy chest would calcify to stone. I ran my hands over the chiseled letters: several Freeloves, clustered on a hill. Some of them were children buried under little rounded stones. The grass was draped into a comb-over beside the newest plot. Downhill, I saw the river braiding currents spawned from narrow sculls, the students pulling oars like windup toys. If Jack walked up, I'd feel him like he was a ripple in the shallow of an ocean that precedes a giant swell. The cemetery was as quiet as a library. I didn't know what time Jack would show up, and so I lay down on the grass and napped. I dreamed about a boy whose chest had turned into a book. There was a front page covering the spot where, once, his heart had clocked the hours of its entombment. I opened up the cover's gilded script and found a singsong fairy tale. It was a song the heart sings fiercely as a swan sings right before its death. A song of accidental beauty, wrapped within the mean of flesh. I dreamed the book had been transplanted for Jack's heart. The thought made me feel in control, when in reality, my nervousness had wrecked me. I had also gotten used to stillness, thinking I would not wake up, so though I heard Jack's clomping boots I didn't open up my eyes. I didn't move for him or look. I felt a nervous breeze of displaced air.

"Hello?" he said. I listened to my breath escaping through my lips. I sounded like a person sucking on a straw.

"Are you alone?" I asked. The cemetery air grew dizzying. I hoped his latest girlfriend wasn't there.

"I broke up with the artist I was dating," said the voice. He reached down and he fanned his fingers through my hair. I felt my roots lift up, his hands of weightless atmospheres. "Her name was Jocelyn. She painted book art, did you hear? Too many words on spines, and yet a paucity of spines supporting words. I hated how we talked but didn't talk."

"I heard about that girl," I said. "I didn't know it ended though. I guess you knew that mine—my last one—ended with a bang."

"I know. It's awful, and I'd like to take you to the water so that I can wash it off of you. What do you think?" said Jack. "I'll carry you. I am the Tin Man after all."

"You really can?"

I felt him mapping out my body's gravity. He scooped his arms under my legs and lifted me against his chest. I wondered if we'd fall into the moss, but then remembered: Jack was healed. I kept my eyes fused shut. I was afraid to look at him. My fabric rubbed against the scar The Sludge had left, which had worn down to chicken-scratch stenography. Jack's arms felt sturdy as two cuts of angle iron. His chest was telling me its backstory—*ka-thump, ka-thump, ka-thump*. Jack's walk had grown more Frankensteinian. He walked the way a movie monster walks, as if his legs were tree trunk shadows that stretched out through city parks. I couldn't open up my eyes. I was afraid he was a chimera of sleep paralysis. We strolled down toward the river, and then Jack said, "Look." I opened up my eyes and focused on two smiling backlit figures standing there. The lighting off the river gave them manes of light.

"This is the actress who played you," said Jack, and pointed to the girly one. "This is the actor who played me."

"Is this one mine?" I turned to him.

"I don't know whose it is," said Jack. "I found them here."

He plunked me on my feet. The girl reached out her

hand to me, but I did not respond. Her black hair was an oily slick against a shore of perfect, rich-girl bones. She wore a sixties superhero too-short skirt and yellow go-go boots. She looked like a hyperbole of me. "Her name's Monique," said Jack. "She is more gorgeous than her head shot. And she's smart. She studied theater at NYU. And his name's Joe. We have to do a gutting ritual before our cleansing ritual. We're going to kill them both."

The trio smiled around the amphitheater of graves, as if exchanging secret thespian proprieties. Joe scratched a chigger bite so that I saw the knife strapped to his leg.

"But why?"

"They are a menace to our memory."

The sun had fled behind a cloud that must have been a sepia diffusing filter. Sudden wind blew whorls of dust off of the chiseled letters. All of the characters sprung into action. "Ain't we a bunch of bandits," Jack drawled. Then he pulled the gun out of his holster. "Yeeaw!" He pointed it at trees and headstones. I loathed these boyish games. I'd been circuitously lassoed once again. "Why can't you put your hobby horse back in your pants?" I snapped, and rolled my eyes. "How many times can one create an outlaw ethic, Jack? There's no one hunting you."

I tried to grab his sleeve as Monique and her boy accomplice dodged behind the tombs. Jack held the gun beyond my reach and mocked me with it, twirling it around his finger. I couldn't stand the giddy absence on his face. I looked away, but he was beaming crazily, so happy to be fighting with these phantoms, to destroy.

"Peeeyow! Pow!" he said, and acted like he shot his gun. "Just play along with us. It's fun."

But suddenly, the day turned sinister. I heard a ting beside me and I saw the shrapnel of a headstone breaking off, the flying bits of stone that barely spared my skin. The stunned air amplified my hunted breath.

PEGGY MUNSON

Monique was glaring at me down the barrel of her gun. She started inching slowly through the brush, her perfect hair unruffled by the fight.

"I'm not a fan of murder-suicide," scowled Jack. "But we have got to make it look that way. We've got to make it look like one of them killed one of them."

I ducked behind a grave for cover. Yes, Monique resembled me, and Joe resembled Jack. Were they just makeup and fake noses? Were they alter-personalities? I was the only one without a gun. Jack guarded me with his and skulked around the stones. I held my hands over my ears, but then I heard the sound inside, the echo that seemed constant since my skull had broken open. My thoughts were cavernous, no more defined than yawns.

Monique crept up behind and ambushed me. She pinned me in her grasp and started dragging me away from Jack, her barrel-end of gun inside my ear so that I couldn't hear my yelps. I felt pathetic when I shirked away from violence now. The Sludge had trained me well. I kicked and thrashed and tried to fend her off. She hauled me back into the shallow of the river, where the crude cartoonish plants hid rusty cans. She pulled her gun away to muscle me onto all fours so I was lapping up the foamy river water. "Baptize me in blood," she said, and shoved my face into the froth. She aimed her gun. I waved my hands in protest. "Yeah, that's right, bitch, tell me who's your inner critic now?" she snarled. "Who tells you when it's time to kill the story line? I am the mistress of the fictioneer. I say The End when it's the end."

"Don't shoot," I yelled. "We are a lot the same. Just look at us."

"It's kill or be killed here," she said, and cocked the safety back. "We're not the same. We're not, you cripple, *not.*"

Just then I heard a bang, but it was not directed at my flesh. There was a little pop. Monique's chest splattered into inky black. Her mouth contorted and I watched her dip her fingers in her chest and smear it on her face. I waited for her body to collapse and make a splash. She wasn't dropping over dead and suddenly, her mouth looked like necrosis. "Blood, you told me blood. And wait—what is this? Ink?" she said in prima-donna snarl. She started stomping through the water, spitting. "Ink!" she screamed. "You cheap shits couldn't even spring for squibs? You couldn't find mortician's wax? Christ, this is amateur."

I reached out, and I dipped one finger in her chest. Indeed, her bra was leaking ink, not blood. Her long legs cut their way across the current and she lunged for Jack, whose gun was smoking still. But Joe was sidling toward Jack and brandishing his .45. "I've got an underground motel for you, Jack-boy," Joe screamed and tried to fire. "It's check-in time."

I saw Joe's finger squeeze and heard his click that didn't turn into a bang. The actors were sophomorically inept. Monique had lost her grip, and I was panning through the water for her gun. Joe and Monique were huddling tight, with Joe's defective gun, and Jack aimed once, then twice, and fired at each of them. Monique let out a little pipsqueak scream and that was it. This time, Joe broke into a thousand paper shards and Monique splattered on him, inking up his parts. They were a pile of inked-up paper shards. Their broken book lay on the ground. Our broken book. The actors who played us within their gutted scripts. Another epilogue before our story was complete.

I crouched to try and make some sense of all the pieces on the ground. I touched the inkblots Monique left.

Jack looked maniacal. He held the weapon in his hand and didn't know if he should go for broke or not. He pointed it at me then at himself. *Scene II: Jack is a homi-cidal suicidal maniac. He is a danger to himself and others.*

Call for help.

"When will it stop?" I asked. "When will we quit destroying everything?"

The edge of water separated us. We each controlled a stage of individual topography. It seemed a good time for soliloquy, but I had nothing eloquent to say. I only wanted to talk plainly, tell him that I loved him still. But looking at him, I began to wonder who he was, and if I even knew him, or myself. I couldn't speak the simple truth. Jack bent down by the scraps of paper and he picked them up. "Amorphous conversation," Jack said. "All of it. And nothing stays in place. I'm done with all the slippage. Nothing ever gets conveyed. I want to die. That's all."

He put the gun into his mouth. This must have been why he had come. To kill himself in front of me. To make me see the Technicolor truth. I couldn't hold him here.

"I want to know you, Jack," I said. "Don't leave me. Please."

As soon as I spoke openly, the scene in front of me lost tracking. It sputtered past my eyes the way a sitcom does when TV sets need smacking on the side.

"You're brrrrr-eaaakk-innnggg uppppp," I said as he was raked into opposing lines. "Come baaaaaa-cccc-kkkk." His lips turned into ribbon candy and they wobbled out some words I couldn't understand.

I shook my head to clear the fuzziness. I thought it must be coma vision, something lingering from head trauma. I couldn't keep Jack's face in focus. I slapped my head to make the visual impairment stop. Jack drew the gun out of his mouth to speak.

"You see? You cannot even know *yourself.* You're leaking everywhere. Your head is in a television set," said Jack. "Your arms are rolled-up magazines. You have to get out of the water now. Come on."

I did exactly what Jack ordered me to do, but as I walked, I saw the pools of ink that floated by, small blobs that touched my clothes and stained them on my way. Jack beckoned me to hurry up. The sky was growing overcast. The tombstones were sprayed out like teeth after a fight, at random places on the ground. It was exactly as I feared: the fictions had lost all delineation once again. The ink was spreading through the sky. The actors who had played us in so many wonderful old scenes became a mangled book. The book was giving in to simple wind. And we were not ourselves again. Already, our reunion had veered toward catastrophe.

"Enough," I shouted. "Jack, just look at me. Just look me in the eyes. Let's be ourselves together. Please."

He looked at me directly for a moment, then his eyes rolled back inside his head. The whites filled up with inky broth. A little triangle of white appeared within the center of the ink that said, "Not this time. Try again." I grabbed him by the shoulders and I shook him.

"Jack!" I screamed. "Don't leave it up to fortune. Talk to me."

The triangle rolled back and reappeared. "It's looking good!" it said.

I shook again. Another triangle. "Stop shaking up the magic ball!" it said.

"Quit doing that," I said. "Just stop." I lightly slapped his head.

"Purge out your perjury!" the triangle said. "Purge out your purgatory!"

Then I held his shoulders squarely, and I hugged him to my chest. I felt his heart in there—*ka-thump, ka-thump*.

"Oh, Jack," I said.

I tried to shake his eyes back into eyes. I wanted him to simply look at me. I thought if we could just connect, see eye to eye, we'd be okay. The triangles kept floating up with messages. "The outlook isn't good!" his right eye said. And "Absolutely not!" he left eye said. I knew I had to do the thing he wanted me to do. I grabbed the hand that held the gun and wrestled out its metal. "Is this the only way to make it end?" I asked, and watched his white eyes nod.

The metal landed in my palm, its certain heft. I pointed at Jack's head, then looked off at a line of trees. It struck me that the metal felt more certain than my minerals inside, or than the minerals beneath my feet. I sighed. I knew that something had to break. Jack had to die. "That's right," he said. His voice was goading me. "When I say pull, you pull."

"If you want this to end, I'll blow your head across the water to the factories," I said. "I'll turn you into waste. Is that what it will take?"

He took a sigh. "Thank you," he said. "Thank God." His eyes resumed their places. "Pull it, baby. Pull."

I skewed my aim and took a practice shot into the woods. Then quickly, I swung back into position. Yes, Jack had to die. I squinted shut one eye and planned my shot. *Let's go,* I told myself. But suddenly, I balked. I don't know if it was the hawk that signaled me to stop. The hawk I saw out of the corner of my eyes, who swooped down after twilight prey. For just a moment, I thought maybe I had walked into a con. My arm was stiff and pointing at his head, but I just couldn't pull. Instead, I looked at him and dropped my trigger arm. I beamed at him.

"I love you, Jack," I said. I raised my arm again. "If you are sure, I'll do it now." My eyes were filling up with tears.

My stalling made Jack angry, and he started hazing me. "Just do it, bitch. What is your fucking problem? Any monkey could. Just pull the trigger, pull. Just waste me. Why can't you redeem your small, pathetic, wasted life and shoot?"

I hated disappointing him. I couldn't do the simplest thing. I couldn't make his awful life erase. I had made everything impossible, by wanting him to be too much, and he was right: I had to be the one to kill him off. I closed my eyes. I squeezed my trigger finger, heard the bang. I slowly pried my eyelids open. I had missed.

"I'm sorry, Jack," I said. My arm dropped limply at my side. I started crying spastically. "I can't." He stormed up, and he fought me for the gun, but I resisted him and wrenched away.

"What's wrong with you? Why would you want to die? Survivor guilt?" I yelled. "You won the lottery! You're better now."

"I guess I've got the misery of millionaires," said Jack. "I'm nouveau riche but I can't stand the eyes of all those presidents."

"I'd *kill* to have your luck," I yelled, and backed away from him. "You know I would."

"So kill. I never asked for anything," said Jack. "But this *one thing.*" He pleaded with me. "Do it for me. Please. I *need* to end. That's all I've ever wanted — just to end." The anguish curled around his lips. "Time's unendurable sometimes," he said.

The clouds were being battered with long sticks and suddenly, a rain came pouring out of them, along with colored hail that looked like sugared candy dots that peel from paper sheets. The bones were rattling beneath the ground to find their way to dry spots in the earth. The hawk I'd watched a moment earlier was carrying a mouse away within its talons and its beak caught on the fabric of the sky. I saw the snagged and thrashing bird. It looked exactly like a fish caught on a line. The candy hail was making a percussive noise as it hit rock and bone. I felt a migraine coming on. I put my hand up to my aching piece of skull that felt — since I'd been struck — like something in a roof that wasn't fully mended. Then suddenly, Jack took one hand and placed it on the leaking spot upside my head. His anger turned to tenderness. "Is this where you were hit?" he asked. He gently rubbed my head. This had distracted him, thank God, so that he didn't see the things I saw. I saw the hawk's beak tugging at the gray beside a cloud, to free itself from where its beak was hooked: the threat of fraying thread. Just when I thought the sky would split apart, the hawk's beak pulled away and left a tiny hole but not a rip. A blue string hung down briefly like a tail of kite and then it floated off, away from us. I hoped Jack didn't see how close the animal had come to ripping up the fragile awning of our lives.

"Feel it. There is a door of bone," I said. I moved his hand to where the ridge of skull was palpable.

"A door? You really have a door of bone? A gentleman would hold it open then," said Jack. "Or shut? I'll hold it shut." He had forgotten all about his will to die. His voice was cheerful, suddenly, with purpose.

"Hold it shut," I said. Then, cheekily: "And in the rain, umbrella me. Umbrella me to seal the leak."

"I will," said Jack. "If that will help. If that is what you want. I will umbrella you right here."

He pulled his jacket over us into a tent that covered both our heads. He narrowed us into a tiny space and then, for once, we met. We lined up evenly beneath the fragile awning, walking slowly toward the shelter of a tree. I tried to see him as he was, beneath that promissory green that seemed too much, too vivid for our eyes. I tried to see him as a heart. I lifted up my fingers and I traced his lips.

"Why am I here again?" Jack asked.

"You are my bodyguard," I said. "You need to let me out and hold me in." I thought that it was something he could handle, just the canopy of one small duty keeping out the rest.

"That's something, isn't it?" asked Jack. "I have a use?" His voice was meek and insecure. He tapped his toes against a tree. He looked so orphaned when he shed his inner strangleholds. He wanted me to give him Pop Psych wisdom—till the garden, man the ferry, Zen those thoughts away. He wanted me to pull him from the ledge and soft-speak him back home. It was not as cementitious as we wanted it to be, but we were mast-lashed and storm-lashed and held whatever we could hold.

"It's more than that," I said. I smiled at him. "It's so much more." I felt the words roll out of me and watched his eyes, to see if he was thinking suicide. I noted the orbicular construction that could flip an hourglass from half-full to empty and then back again. We kept on top-pling through perception. "Just stay here," I said. "Please stay."

He caught the candy hail by handfuls, and he put it on my tongue. My simpleton solution gave him a dis-tracted peace. Then Jack was looking elsewhere, not at me, and that's when I broke off from him, just long enough to slip his handgun in my purse. I felt its warmth against my hip, the warmth that soon would turn to cold. He'd ask me later where it was, and I would tell him that I'd buried it as quickly as I could inside the clay along the riverbank. I'd claim I salvaged out the clay the gun displaced. I'd show it to him — look, a bowl, a teapot, some utilitarian result — and he'd believe I made it from the clay. But this would be my biggest fib. Instead, I'd sleep on metal every night, the gun beneath our mat-tress. Not an albatross, but something small and hardly sinister, a pea, a tiny private piece. We'd both sleep slightly cocked and lie about it later.

I wish I could be strong enough to throw the gun away. I wish I didn't keep insurance nestled underneath my dreams. For years after that day, I shifted aching bones around so that I wouldn't feel the pistol, how it slept beneath me like a small bent leg. But honestly, the war I planted was the only thing that let me know I was a princess and I had my pea. I heard the echo of the future in the chamber of that unused force. We all need something to believe in and a thing to struggle up against. I knew that Jack and I could only handle love if we knew how its final shot might sound.

Ka-thump, I slept against the only metronome we had to keep ourselves in unity and check. *Ka-thump.* That foreign heart was all we really had.

Peggy Munson has published in books such as the *Best American Poetry 2003*, *On Our Backs: The Best Erotic Fiction*, *Genderqueer*, *Pinned Down by Pronouns*, *Hers3: Brilliant New Fiction by Lesbian Writers*, *Tough Girls*, *Best Bisexual Erotica 2*, *Best Lesbian Erotica* editions *1998-2005*, and both editions of the *Best of Best Lesbian Erotica*. She is the editor of *Stricken: Voices from the Hidden Epidemic of Chronic Fatigue Syndrome*. She has published in periodicals such as *Literature and Medicine*, *On Our Backs*, the *San Francisco Bay Guardian*, *Blithe House Quarterly*, *Margin: Exploring Modern Magical Realism*, *Lodestar Quarterly*, *Spoon River Poetry Review*, *13th Moon*, and *Sinister Wisdom*. She has been awarded literary fellowships by the MacDowell Colony, Cottages at Hedgebrook, and the Ragdale Foundation. She has been a finalist or semifinalist for many prizes, including the Dorset Prize, Astraea Grant, Beatrice Hawley Award, *Spoon River Poetry Review* Editor's Prize, and Tupelo Press First Book Competition. She was a winner of the *San Francisco Bay Guardian* Fiction Contest and the Project: QueerLit contest. A graduate of Oberlin College and a Midwest native, Peggy now lives amongst pine trees in New England. She has been disabled by Chronic Fatigue Immune Dysfunction Syndrome (CFIDS) and Multiple Chemical Sensitivity (MCS) for over a decade, and devotes most of her energy to healing and raising awareness about these disabilities. Peggy considers herself queer in many ways—she is an exile from chemical culture, a poet in a capitalist economy, a writer of cerebral erotica, and a dyke out of Normal, Illinois. More on Peggy and her work can be found at www.peggymunson.com.

Pink Steam by Dodie Bellamy. $16.95, 0-9746388-0-3. A collection from the author of *The Letters of Mina Harker* and *Cunt-Ups*. *Pink Steam* reveals the intimate secrets of Dodie Bellamy's life — sex, shoplifting, voyeurism, writing. "Bellamy is David Lynch in print, teen porn under fluorescent lights, a sandpaper jumpsuit sandy side in." — Lynn Breedlove

Pulling Taffy by Matt Bernstein Sycamore. $16.95, 0-9710846-3-7. Moving from mid-nineties Boston, to post-grunge Seattle, to Giuliani's New York, *Pulling Taffy* inhabits the boundaries between fiction, autobiography, and truth. "I admire the candor and the reticence in this beautiful, anguished, funny novel. I have seen the future and it is *Pulling Taffy*." — Edmund White

Satyriasis: Literotica² by Ian Philips. $16.95, 0-9710846-5-3. From the award-winning author of *See Dick Deconstruct* comes a new collection of literotica that leaves no prodigal son unspanked and no udder of any sacred cow untweaked. "In this madcap, pansexual, and polymorphous perverse collection of short stories, everybody has to pay the piper." — Patrick Califia

Supervillainz by Alicia E. Goranson. $16.95, 0-9763411-8-2. Rump-smacking good action-adventure trans fiction that boots transgender literature out of the classroom. A hard-edged tale of passion, revenge, and low-rent apartments, *Supervillainz* has romance, car chases, brutal superheroes, epic battles in dyke bars, and a climax that will have you reaching for the tissues.

Toilet by Thomas Woolley, foreword by D. Travers Scott. $12.95, 0-9763411-2-3. "Both cheery and cantankerous, the stories and rantings of *Toilet* are linked by a battery-acid tone and a smart, atomic energy. Thomas Woolley is a wholly engaging original, and injects his humor with equal parts horror and sad, eerie nostalgia." — Scott Heim

For more information on Suspect Thoughts Press and our authors and titles or to request a free catalog and to order directly from us, visit our website at www.suspectthoughtspress.com.

Select Titles
from Suspect Thoughts Press
"The queerest little press on earth."

The Beautifully Worthless by Ali Liebegott. $12.95, 0-9746388-4-6. A brilliant novel in verse about a runaway waitress and her Dalmatian, Rorschach, who leave Brooklyn on a postmodern odyssey through an American landscape to find hope in a town named Camus, Idaho. "Ali Liebegott is just what the world of books needs...I do believe she is a genius..." — Michelle Tea

Bullets & Butterflies: queer spoken word poetry, edited by Emanuel Xavier. $16.95, 0-9746388-5-4. Features vibrant, sexy, and shocking new poetry by Cheryl Boyce-Taylor, Regie Cabico, Staceyann Chin, Celena Glenn, Daphne Gottlieb, Maurice Jamal, Shane Luitjens, Marty McConnell, Travis Montez, Alix Olson, Shailja Patel, and horehound stillpoint.

Burn by Jennifer Natalya Fink. $16.95, 0-9710846-8-8. Set amidst the sexual and political repression of the 1950s, Burn tells the story of the flamboyant Sylvia Edelman and Sylvan Lake, a socialist Jewish colony in northern Westchester. A fable for the Bush/Rumsfeld era, Burn will scorch the reader with its Faulkneresque tale of tomatoes, torture, and tangled love.

Killing Me Softly: Morir Amando by Francisco Ibáñez-Carrasco. $16.95, 0-9746388-1-1. Twelve genre-blurring and gender-bending tales from the author of *Flesh Wounds and Purple Flowers*. "If you scraped the rainbow paint off your pride rings with a dirty thumbnail, you would find Francisco's world, skillfully rendered and beautifully imperfect." — Ivan E. Coyote

One of These Things Is Not Like the Other by D. Travers Scott. $16.95, 0-9746388-6-2. Suicide, homicide, fratricide, incest — it's a love story. A thriller from the author of *Execution, Texas: 1987*. "...[S]urreally incestuous brothers and sexy parapsychological polymorphs...a jagged and multifaceted backwater noir, filled with revelation and life." — Stephen Winter